Born Pauline Mary Tarn in Lond
and American mother, Renée V
and moved to Paris permanently
fortune at the age of 21. She lived
expatriate lesbian set and had re
including the American writer Natalie Clifford Barney and the
Rothschild heiress Baroness Hélène van Zuylen de Nyevelt,
to whom *The Woman of the Wolf* is believed to be dedicated.
Vivien was a prolific writer of often autobiographical poetry
and prose in the French language and became established as one
of the finest second-generation Symbolists. Her reworkings of
traditional myths and fairy tales prefigure the modern trend for
feminist retellings. She was the subject of a pen-portrait by her
friend and neighbour Colette, published after Vivien's death in
1909 at the age of thirty-two.

Karla Jay is an award-winning author, activist and academic. She
is a distinguished professor emerita at Pace University, where she
taught English Literature and directed the women's and gender
studies programme.

Yvonne M. Klein is a retired college teacher and an award-winning
translator. She was professor of English at Dawson College in
Montreal, where she taught courses in women's literature and
Modernism. Her translation of Jovette Marchessault's Lesbian
Triptych was awarded the Governor General's Prize for best
English translation.

Also available in the Revolutionary Women series:

Three Rival Sisters by Marie-Louise Gagneur

Asphyxia by Violette Leduc

THE WOMAN OF THE WOLF

and other stories

RENÉE VIVIEN

Translated by Karla Jay & Yvonne M. Klein
Adapted by Gallic Books

Gallic Books
London

A Gallic Book

First published in the USA in 1983 by Gay Presses of New York
English translation copyright © 1983, Karla Jay and Yvonne M. Klein
Introduction © 1983, Karla Jay

First published in Great Britain in 2020 by Gallic Books,
59 Ebury Street, London, SW1W 0NZ

'The Veil of Vashti' appeared in *Sojourner*, Vol. 5, No. 12
(August 1980). Copyright © 1980 by Karla Jay.
Karla Jay would like to thank the Gay Academic Union for their
scholarship which encouraged her to continue research into the work
of Natalie Clifford Barney and Renée Vivien. She would also like
to thank Mgt. Desmond for her devoted help and support on this
project.
A CIP record for this book is available from the British Library
ISBN 9781910477946

Typeset by Gallic Books

Printed in the UK by CPI (C20 4YY)

Dedicated to my friend

H. L. C. B.[1]

INTRODUCTION

The Woman of the Wolf and Other Stories, written in 1904, is probably Renée Vivien's finest achievement, the one work in which she combines powerful characters and exciting narratives with the poetic clarity of style and vision so apparent in her other works. In this collection of short stories and prose poems, Vivien manages to touch on all the themes and ideas which obsessed her throughout her short life.

Though some of Vivien's other works, including *A Woman Appeared to Me* ... , are gynocentric – that is, place women at the core of human experience – it is in *The Woman of the Wolf* that her stance is most explicit. For example, 'The Veil of Vashti' takes two well-known biblical tales – the stories of Lilith and of Vashti – and recreates them so that these women are no longer peripheral figures but become central ones. In the Bible the rebellious Lilith is merely a preface to the story of the obedient Eve as the disobedient Vashti precedes the faithful Esther. Here, however, Vashti and Lilith not only take centre stage, but they are also transformed from evil figures into heroic ones. Vashti is, as Elizabeth Cady Stanton said of her in *The Woman's Bible*, the epitome of 'self-centred womanhood'. In 'White as Foam', the same transformation is wrought on Andromeda, originally rescued by Perseus, almost as an afterthought, on his return from other conquests. In Vivien's version, Andromeda prefers solitude and death to Perseus's embrace.

At the heart of these transformations lies a startlingly radical core of perception about the profound antagonism between the psyches of men and women and about the potentialities of women sprung loose from conventional stereotypical behaviour. These themes appear most clearly in the group of short stories which are told from the point of view of male narrators, of which the title story is one.

In Renée Vivien's view, men are not merely contemptuous or patronising towards women: they are positively murderous. All of them are locked in a self-protective, impregnable egotism, which assumes a kind of gender solidarity from other men and which demands passive support from all women. When this support is withheld – or worse, when their smug self-satisfaction is challenged by women who refuse to accede to their demands – the men turn killer.

In the title story, for example, the narrator regales a mixed after-dinner party with the tale of an extraordinary woman he remembers from a shipwreck. Throughout the course of his story, he turns again and again to the men present for confirmation that his notion of the innate flirtatiousness of women is correct. No one interrupts with an objection. He presents his portrait of a woman who prefers a pure death in the sea in the company of her pet wolf to the 'normal' existence he has implicitly offered her as an oddity; he never understands what motivates the heroine. But if a normal existence consists of sexual connection with this monster of egotism, the reader is with the heroine all the way to the bottom of the sea.

The heroine of 'The Woman of the Wolf' challenges the narrator simply through her aloof indifference to his dubious sexual charms; in the two stories set in a rather Gallic version of the American wilderness, the challenge is more aggressive. The heroine of 'Sniggering Thirst', Polly, is infinitely more competent and assured than the narrator. The traditional roles here are almost completely reversed. The narrator maintains he is 'slightly more intelligent' than his companion on the American prairies, but the reader is given no evidence to support this. In the face of almost certain death, he becomes a quivering mass of jelly, incapable of action but consumed with hatred of Polly for her fearlessness. Polly, on the other hand, conforms to the ideal of the male hero of adventure fiction. A 'gentle giant', she is a hard-drinking woman of few words, but of effective action. Her prompt initiative, which rescues them from immediate death, generates no gratitude in the narrator; on the contrary, he hates her the more for her capability and continues to plot her death. For him, indeed, the only good woman is a dead one: he dreams throughout the story of an unnamed woman from his youth with a pale face whose very passivity, the reader suspects, led her to an early grave, perhaps assisted by the narrator.

The superior woodcraft of the heroine of 'The Nut-Brown Maid' is also instrumental in saving the two characters. Although the relationship between Nell and Jerry in this story is somewhat more egalitarian than in most of the others, the heroine still displays a spirited defiance of Jerry's sexual demands on her. Even in the face of death, she spurns Jerry's maudlin pleas for a quick kiss.

Some of this extreme behaviour will seem comic to many, and the intent is clearly so. After reading the satirical commentary of a wry story such as 'The Saurienne', those who have misconstrued Renée Vivien as a lugubrious writer obsessed with death will be pleasantly surprised.

Readers of all ages will be enchanted with tales such as 'Prince Charming', in which Vivien takes a fresh approach to old themes and deftly destroys all the fairy-tale nonsense on which most of us were raised.

Vivien's genius lies precisely in reworking the material around her, whether it is a biblical story such as 'The Friendship of Women', a popular adventure story such as 'Forest Betrayal', or a Greek or Roman tale such as 'Bona Dea'. In the last, for example, Vivien compiles a number of Sappho's fragments into a prose poem about the rites of spring. Sappho's love for Atthis ('Atthis, I loved you long ago while you still seemed to me a small ungracious child') is transformed into a mistress's love for her slave, Amata ('You were but a sickly and graceless child'). Just as Sappho freed Atthis to pursue Andromeda (a rival poet), the narrator liberates Amata for the Goddess and other women.

In other words, Vivien feels most comfortable beginning with familiar models, whether it is Sappho or a popular Symbolist theme such as chastity. Then she transforms them so that they take on new perspectives and meanings. Whereas traditional female figures such as Sara in Villiers de l'Isle-Adam's *Axël* are chaste from a deep-rooted and unalterable frigidity, Vivien's heroines are virgins because they are defiant and disdain men, and in some cases because they are lesbians.

Vivien's weaknesses stem from the same source – that is, using the models provided for her by others. In the Romantic mode, Vivien often chooses settings that are exotic, improbable or bizarre. Her stories take place in Africa, on the high seas, in Renaissance Italy, ancient Greece or the plains of North America. It soon becomes apparent how little Vivien knows of certain periods of history or of life in the wild. Vivien would probably argue that she hardly means for the reader to take her stories literally. Vivien is not primarily concerned with the real world as we might recognise it. Her fantastic universe majestically floats several feet above the ground, never anchored firmly to reality by factual accuracy or believability. Rather, Vivien is concerned with the embedded meanings and deep symbolism, which she clothes in the gaudy colours of faraway places and distant times.

Even within the terms of her created world, Vivien displays many of the limitations of her class and situation. She is an elitist, admiring a small number of highly favoured women whose circumstances have permitted them to withdraw altogether from economic and social reality to pursue lives of aesthetic purity. She is frequently suspicious of sexuality, though she recognises its force. She exhibits the unconscious and unwitting racism and anti-Semitism of the white Anglo-Saxon of her period. If judged from a contemporary lesbian/feminist perspective, some of Vivien's work might appear embarrassing.

Again, Vivien lived in a world of poetic reality, not political reality, and it would be harsh to judge her on terms she didn't even think in. She was more concerned with the manner in which the story was told than the plot. Indeed, her talent partially lies in the fact that she managed to offer radically different alternatives to the deceptively familiar myth or adventure story. In other words, one might suggest that the smoothness of her finished work shields the complex imagery and poetic philosophy that went into the construction of it, much as Vivien often tried to hide the effort that went into her craft by pretending it was raw and unrefined inspiration.

The woman behind the stories is equally complex. Born Pauline Mary Tarn in London in 1877, she moved to Paris at the turn of the century and wrote in French. She was considered one of the best second-generation Symbolist poets of France, though French was not her native tongue. Despite the fact that she died in 1909 in her thirty-second year, she wrote over ten volumes of poetry, several prose poems, some plays and two novels (one unfinished). Three of her works – *A Woman Appeared to Me* ..., *The Muse of the Violets* and *At the Sweet Hour of Hand in Hand* – appeared in English for the first time in the 1970s from Naiad Press.

In her earliest works, Vivien pretended she was a man by writing under the name R. Vivien or René Vivien; but in 1903 she began to sign her works Renée Vivien, thus making it clear that she was a woman. She soon became known as the Sappho of her era because of the explicitly lesbian nature of her love poems.

Shortly after she began writing, Vivien became involved with Natalie Clifford Barney, the renowned 'Amazon', who was later noted for her many lovers and for her salon (which began in 1909), to which all the intellectuals of Europe flocked. Barney was also a writer and the most flamboyant lesbian seductress of perhaps any era (her conquests included Liane de Pougy, Romaine Brooks, Dolly Wilde and many other well-known women of the period who lived in Paris). Vivien's liaison with Barney has been widely discussed, including in two biographies about Barney: George Wickes's *The Amazon of Letters* and Jean Chalon's *Portrait of a Seductress*. Djuna Barnes also wrote a book, *Ladies Almanack*, about Barney and her conquests.

Vivien is notable for her enterprises as well as for her writing and love affair with Barney, for Vivien (like Barney) felt it was not enough to have a good idea: one had to *live* it as well. In 1904 Vivien and Barney travelled on the Orient Express to Constantinople; from there they went by boat to Lesbos, where they decided they would set up an artists' colony for lesbian poets. They first invited English poet Olive Custance, with whom they had both been involved, to join them, but the colony never materialised, for Vivien's other lover, the Baroness Hélène van Zuylen de Nyevelt (one of the most powerful noblewomen in Europe) came to 'reclaim' Vivien.

Though Barney and Vivien were never reunited, this adventure shows in part why Vivien is the kind of woman around whom myths and legends are made. She was the subject of curiosity for many of her contemporaries, including Colette, whose wonderful portrait of her next-door neighbour Vivien in *The Pure and the Impure* captures some of Vivien's withdrawal from the world after her separation from Barney, her fascination with the Orient, her mysterious method for creating poems (no one really saw her write), her mysterious love affair (with a woman who never appeared before others) and her mysterious death (some suggest she died of anorexia, others of alcoholism – and perhaps it was a combination of both). Perhaps even her death was part of her belief that she should reify her ideas – in this case, the beauty of death. Its circumstances also created another mystery: whether or not Vivien converted to Catholicism before she died in order to be reunited with her first love, Violet Shillito, whose death in 1901 left Vivien inconsolable and from which she never fully recovered.

During her life Vivien dreamed of creating a new golden age of Sappho – first on the island of Lesbos and then in her writing – in which the principles of the divine tenth muse would be enacted, a world in which the goodness and the courage of women would be praised and recounted, a world in which the evil values of the patriarchy would be overturned. More than a century after Vivien's death, we still do not have the world she envisioned, but this translation of Vivien's defining work tries to capture her spirit. Now all may know why this highly praised writer is so much discussed and written about and why her memory, like that of her beloved Sappho, is still cherished.

— *Karla Jay*

CONTENTS

Contents

THE WOMAN OF THE WOLF

Narrated by M. Pierre Lenoir, 69, rue des Dames, Paris

I do not know why I undertook to court that woman. She was neither beautiful, nor pretty, nor even agreeable. As for myself (and I say this without conceit, dear ladies), there are those who have not been indifferent to me. It is not that I am extraordinarily endowed by nature, physically or mentally, but simply – may I confess it? – that I have been spoiled when it comes to the fairer sex. Oh, do not be alarmed: I am not going to inflict upon you a vain recital of my conquests. I am a modest man. In any case, this story is not about me. It is about a particular woman, or rather, a particular young lady, an Englishwoman, whose strange face enchanted me for an hour or so.

She was a peculiar specimen. When I approached her for the first time, a great beast was sleeping in the trailing folds of her skirt. I had on my lips the amiably banal remarks that break the ice between strangers. Words mean nothing in such cases; the art of pronouncing them is everything … But the great beast, lifting its muzzle, growled ominously just as I reached the interesting stranger.

I drew back a step, despite myself. 'You have quite a vicious dog there, mademoiselle,' I observed.

'It is a she-wolf,' she replied, somewhat sharply. 'And since she sometimes turns on people, violently and inexplicably, I think you would do well to step back a bit.' With one stern word, she silenced the wolf: 'Helga!'

I left, somewhat humiliated. It was a stupid business, you must admit. Fear is foreign to me, but I hate ridicule. The incident bothered me all the more since I thought I had seen a glimmer of liking in the young lady's eye. I certainly pleased her somewhat. She must have been as vexed as I at this regrettable setback. What a pity! A conversation that had been so promising at the outset …

I do not know why the frightful animal later ceased its display of hostility. I was able to approach its mistress without fear. I had never seen such a strange face. Her pale grey complexion glowed white under heavy blonde hair, which was both fiery and colourless, like burning ashes. Her emaciated body had the fine and fragile delicacy of a lovely skeleton. (We are all a little artistic in Paris, you see.) This woman radiated an impression of tough and solitary pride, of flight and of fierce recoil. Her yellow eyes resembled those of her she-wolf. They both wore an expression of sly hostility. Her footsteps were so silent that they became disturbing. No one had ever walked so quietly. She was dressed in a thick material which looked like fur. She was neither beautiful, nor pretty, nor charming. But she was the only woman on board the ship.

So, I courted her. I played by rules based on my already extensive experience. She had the intelligence not to let me see the deep pleasure my advances afforded her. Even her yellow eyes maintained their usual mistrustful expression. A remarkable example of feminine wiles! This only made me more violently attracted to her. Drawn-out resistance sometimes leads to a pleasant surprise, rendering the victory all the more brilliant …

You would not contradict me on this point, would you, gentlemen? We all share the same sentiments to some degree. There is such complete fraternity of spirit between us that conversation is almost impossible. That is why I often flee the monotonous company of men – they are too identical to myself.

Admittedly, the Woman of the Wolf attracted me. And furthermore – dare I confess it? – the enforced chastity of that floating jail made my feelings yet more turbulent. She was a woman ... and my courting of her, respectful until then, became each day more insistent. I built up blazing metaphors. I elegantly elaborated eloquent expressions.

Look at the extent of the woman's deceitfulness! In listening to me, she adopted an air of moonstruck distraction. One would have sworn she was interested only in the foaming wake which looked like steaming snow. (Women are by no means indifferent to flowery similes.) But I, who had long studied the feelings behind the feminine face, understood that her heavy, lowered eyelids concealed vacillating glimmers of love.

One day I was particularly bold, combining flattering gestures with delicate words, when she turned to me with the spring of a she-wolf.

'Go away,' she commanded, with almost savage decisiveness. Her teeth, like those of a wild beast, glittered strangely behind lips drawn back in menace.

I smiled, without any anxiety. You must have patience with women, must you not? And you must not believe a single word they say. When they order you to depart, you must remain. Really, gentlemen, I am rather ashamed to give you the same old mediocre banalities.

The lady considered me with her large, yellow eyes. 'You

have not worked me out. You are foolishly running up against my insurmountable contempt. I know neither how to hate nor love. I have not yet met a human worthy of my hatred. Hatred, which is more patient and more tenacious than love, deserves a great adversary.'

She caressed Helga's heavy head. The wolf looked back at her with the deep eyes of a woman. 'And love? I know as little about that as you know about concealing your inherent masculine conceit, a technique which is elementary among us Anglo-Saxons. If I were a man, I would have perhaps loved a woman, for women possess the qualities I value: loyalty in passion and selflessness in affection. In general, women are simple and sincere. They give of themselves without restriction and without counting the cost. Their patience is as inexhaustible as their kindness. They are able to forgive. They are able to wait. They possess a superior kind of chastity: constancy.'

I do not lack finesse and I can take a hint. I smiled meaningfully in response to her outburst of enthusiasm. She gave me a distracted look, taking me in.

'Oh, you are strangely mistaken. I have observed women in passing who are generous in spirit and in heart. But I have never become attached to them. Their very gentleness sets them at a distance from me. My spirit is not sufficiently noble, and so I lose patience in the face of their excessive candour and devotion.'

She was beginning to bore me with her pretentious discourse. A prude and a bluestocking, and a brat too! ... But she was the only woman on board. And she was only putting on airs of superiority to make her imminent capitulation the more precious.

'I have affection for Helga alone. And Helga knows it. As for you, you are probably a nice enough little man, but you cannot imagine how much I despise you.'

By hurting my pride, she was trying to make me want her even more. She was succeeding, too, the little hussy! I was red with anger and lust.

'Men who hover around women, any women, are like dogs sniffing after bitches.' She gave me one of her long yellow looks. 'I have for so long breathed the forest air, air that quivers with snow; I have spent so much time amid vast, barren whiteness, that my soul is not unlike the souls of fleeting she-wolves.'

The woman had finally frightened me. She perceived it and changed her tone. 'I love clarity and freshness,' she continued, with a little laugh. 'Thus, the crudeness of men is as off-putting as the stench of garlic, and their dirtiness as repulsive as the waft of a drain. Men,' she insisted, 'are only really at home in brothels. They love only courtesans. For in them they discover their own rapacity, their sentimental unintelligence, their stupid cruelty. They live for self-interest and debauchery alone. Morally, they sicken me; physically, I find them repugnant ... I have seen men kissing women on the lips while obscenely fondling them. A gorilla's performance would not have been more repellent.'

She ceased for a minute. 'Even the severest legislator only escapes by a miracle the deplorable consequences of the carnal promiscuity of his youth. I do not understand how even the least sensitive woman could endure your filthy embraces without retching. Indeed, my virgin's contempt is equal in disgust to the courtesan's nausea!'

Really, I thought, *she is overdoing it, though she understands her part very well. She is overdoing it.*

(If we were among ourselves, gentlemen, I would tell you that I have not always despised public houses, and have even picked up a few pitiful whores on the street. Parisian women were nonetheless more accommodating than that hypocrite. I am by no means smug, but one must be aware of one's own worth.)

Deeming that the conversation had gone on long enough, I took dignified leave of the Woman of the Wolf. Helga slyly followed me with her long yellow gaze.

Towering clouds loomed on the horizon. A streak of dull blue-green sky was winding like a moat beneath them. I felt as though I were being crushed between stone walls ... And the wind was getting up ...

I was seized with seasickness – I do beg your pardon for such an inelegant detail, dear ladies. I was horribly indisposed ... I fell asleep around midnight, feeling more pitiful than I could tell you.

Around two o'clock in the morning, I was awakened by a sinister impact, followed by an even more sinister grinding sound. The darkness emitted an inexpressible terror. I realised that the ship had struck a reef. For the first time in my life, I neglected my clothes. I appeared on deck in extremely skimpy attire.

A confused crowd of half-naked men were already swarming about up there. They were hurriedly launching the lifeboats. Looking at those hairy arms and shaggy chests, I could not help remembering, not without a smile, something the Woman of the Wolf had said: '*A gorilla's performance would not have been more repellent ...*' I do not know why that unimportant memory came back to mock me in the midst of the common danger.

The waves looked like monstrous volcanoes wreathed in white

smoke. Or, rather, they looked like nothing at all. They were themselves – magnificent, terrible, mortal ... The wind was blowing across their enormous wrath and so increasing their frenzy. The salt bit at my eyes. I shivered in the spray as though in a cold drizzle, and the crashing of the waves obliterated all my thoughts.

The Woman of the Wolf was calmer than ever. And I was faint with terror. I could see death looming before me. I could almost touch it. I distractedly put my fingers to my forehead, where I could feel the bones of my skull bulging frightfully. The skeleton within me terrified me. Idiotically, I started to cry ...

My flesh would be black and blue, more swollen than a bulging wineskin. The sharks would snap at my dismembered limbs. And, when I sank beneath the waves, the crabs would climb sideways along my rotten corpse and gluttonously eat their fill.

The wind was blowing over the waters ...

I relived my past. I repented my idiotic life, my spoiled life, my lost life. I tried to remember one act of kindness I may have performed, either absent-mindedly or inadvertently. Had I ever been good for anything, useful to anyone? And the dark side of my conscience cried out, as horrifying as a mute who has miraculously recovered his speech: 'No!'

The wind was blowing over the waters ...

I vaguely remembered the sacred words which encourage repentance and which promise salvation to the contrite sinner even at the hour of death. I strove to retrieve from my memory, drier now than an empty goblet, a few words of prayer ... And lustful thoughts came to torment me, like little red devils. I again saw the soiled beds of chance companions. I heard their stupidly obscene cries once more. I re-experienced loveless embraces. I

23

was overwhelmed with the horror of Pleasure ...

Faced with the terror of the Mysterious Immensity, all that survived in me was the rutting instinct, as powerful for some as the instinct of self-preservation. It was Life, crude, ugly Life, screaming its ferocious protest against Annihilation.

The wind was blowing over the waters ...

One has peculiar ideas at times like that, all the same ... There I was – a very decent fellow, admired by all, except for a few who were jealous of me, even loved by some – so bitterly reproaching myself for an existence which was neither better nor worse than anyone else's. I must have succumbed to a moment of madness. We were all a little mad, anyway ...

The Woman of the Wolf was looking out at the white waves, completely calm ... Oh! they were whiter than snow at twilight! And, sitting up on her haunches, Helga was howling like a dog. She howled pitifully, like a dog baying at the moon. She *understood*.

I do not know why her howls chilled me even more than the sound of the wind and the waves. She howled at death, that damned devil-wolf. I wanted to knock her senseless just to shut her up, and I looked for a plank, a spar, an iron bar, anything on the deck to beat her with ... I found nothing.

The lifeboat was finally ready to leave. The men leapt frantically towards salvation. Only the Woman of the Wolf did not move.

'Get in, then,' I shouted at her as I took my turn.

She came slowly over to the boat, followed by Helga.

'Mademoiselle,' said the lieutenant, who was commanding us as well as he could, 'we cannot take that animal with us. There is only enough room for people.'

'In that case, I will stay,' she said, stepping back...

The terror-stricken men rushed forward with incoherent cries. We had to let her stay behind.

I really couldn't be bothered with such a silly girl. And she had been so insolent to me! You understand that, gentlemen, don't you? You would not have acted any differently.

Finally I was saved, or just about. Dawn broke and, my God, what a dawn! There was a shiver of chilling light, a grey stupor, a swarm of people and unformed shapes in a dusky confusion of limbs...

And we saw the blue of distant land...

Oh, what joy and comfort to see the trusty, welcoming sun! ... Since that horrible experience I have only once travelled by sea, and that was to return here. I won't be doing it again, you can be sure of that!

I must not be too egotistical, dear ladies. In the midst of such unspeakable uncertainty, and though I had narrowly escaped Destruction, I was still brave enough to concern myself with the fate of my companions in misfortune. The second lifeboat had been swamped by too many frenzied madmen. With horror, I saw it sink... The Woman of the Wolf had taken refuge on a broken mast, along with her obedient animal. I was quite certain that she would be saved, as long as her strength and endurance did not fail her. I hoped so, with all my heart... But there was the cold, her slow, fragile improvised raft, which lacked sails and rudder, her fatigue, her feminine weakness!

They were not far from land when the Woman, exhausted, turned to Helga, as if to say, 'I am finished...'

And then a most mournful and solemn thing occurred. The she-wolf, *who had understood*, hurled her howl of despair at the close yet inaccessible shore ... Then, standing up, she put her two front paws on the shoulders of her mistress, who took her in her arms. Together, they disappeared beneath the waves.

SNIGGERING THIRST

Narrated by Jim Nichols

'What a peculiar sunset!' I said to Polly.

We were travelling on our mules, which were heavy with heat and weariness.

'Imbecile!' muttered my companion. 'Can't you see that the light is in the east?'

'In that case, it must be dawn. I must be drunk – and yet I haven't had a drink all day.'

The mules' sleepy pace was pleasantly lulling me into daydreams.

We were in the middle of the prairie. In front of us was a desert of pale grass, behind us an ocean of pale grass. Thirst was prowling around us. I could see her dry lips moving. I could hear her shivering with fever. Polly, the bitch with straw-like hair, couldn't see her, which didn't surprise me at all. Polly could never see anything beyond the end of her nose, reddened by the sun and the outdoors.

I turned around in my saddle, drawing sharply on the reins.

'Why are you stopping?' Polly asked.

'I am looking at Thirst. Her dress is as grey as the dry grass down there. She is making a face. She is sniggering. The contortions of her carcass frighten me. She's certainly ugly enough.'

Polly heavily shrugged her heavy shoulders. 'You're crazy,

Jim. Only idiots like you have nightmares in broad daylight.'

I would happily have given her a kick or a punch to shut her up, but too many unpleasant former experiences had convinced me that Polly was far stronger than I. My only advantage was that I was slightly more intelligent. And yet, my companion's good sense had often got me out of bad situations, which my visionary meanderings would never have been able to do.

I was educated, it's true, but what good is an education on the prairies? A good revolver is worth a lot more.

Polly's hair shone defiantly in the light. I had a desire to scalp her, like my friends and enemies the Indians, and spatter that blonde mane of hair with blood. Why? I do not know. That's the kind of thing that suddenly occurs to you on the prairies.

I looked at her tanned cheeks, which resembled two baked apples. I do not know why I was then reminded of a pale, thin face I had once loved. I remembered the shade of a cottage, the coolness of closed shutters and the beautiful eyelids of a girl reading. How charming she was, with her lids lowered! I adored the shadow of her eyelashes on her white cheeks. Ah!

In those days, I knew nothing about being a prairie rider. I hadn't yet met the bitch with straw-like hair.

Why did I leave a cottage full of shade and the green light of closed shutters? I do not know. I do not even know if that odd little girl who would read for hours is alive or dead. I think she must be dead, because sometimes my heart feels so very empty!

But I am not sure of anything.

Seeing Thirst up close, roaming the prairies, disturbs your thoughts a little. I chose Polly, whom I detest, as my travelling companion – or rather, she chose me. I will end up killing her one of these days. I know that, at least. I hate her because she is so robustly healthy, while I am such a feverish weakling. She is more daring and more solid than a man. She could send me flying six feet with a flick of the wrist. But she is a gentle giant, when she hasn't had too much to drink. She does like to get drunk, though. Perhaps she too is afraid of Thirst, who is lying in wait for both of us.

I ventured a comment along the way. 'There'll be a storm before long, Polly, my angel, my dream.'

'Idiot!' she breathed, with feeling. 'Leave me alone. You are always talking nonsense. Of course there'll be a storm before long. You can see it and you can smell it, and I don't care for unnecessary chatter.'

'Oh, my sweet, your wisdom is as kind as it is profound.'

She didn't bother answering me. I will certainly end up killing her one of these days. I will never be strong enough to strangle her, but I will shoot her in the back with a single revolver shot. Then it will all be over and I won't have to think about her any more. Perhaps Thirst will leave me alone once I've showered her with blood. Who knows?

The unnatural light was becoming more intense…

We came to a halt when dusk fell. Polly poured me a drop of liquor from her bulging waterskin. I drank to her early death. All of a sudden, the bitch stopped drinking. That surprised me a little. Only something truly extraordinary could have distracted Polly from the great pleasure of her favourite beverage.

'What's the matter?' I asked, with affectionate interest.

Polly hates unnecessary chatter, I'll give her that. Her long journeys under the sun have made her taciturn. She really is the perfect companion for a man of the prairies. She simply gestured to a few ashes in the grey grass.

29

I knew what she was thinking. I looked instinctively towards the peculiar dawn which was glowing red in the east. But a little hill prevented me from seeing what was happening over there.

Polly spat a muffled curse. My knees buckled under me. She looked me scornfully up and down and, without saying a word, she left me and set off to climb the little hill. I followed her, for I feared being left alone even more than I detested her company.

We reached the top, gasping for breath. From north to south, the entire horizon was a blazing inferno. A prairie fire! A wind of flame, which hits you at the speed of a simoom or a sirocco and sweeps over the desert of dry grass in the blink of an eye. And nothing in its way to stop it!

I shook like a sick man dying of fever. But Polly was not at all afraid.

For a minute, I almost forgot my own dread in my fury at finding that she was not scared. Her terror would almost have calmed my own fears. But she is brave, much braver than I am. She did not turn pale, because nothing in the world, not even death or the sound of the Last Judgement would make her turn pale. She has a particularly ruddy complexion anyway. I, on the other hand, was yellower than a guinea.

We returned as quickly as possible to our makeshift camp, where we had left our mules grazing. Fear had made them bad-tempered. The evening breeze was sending the hurricane of flames in our direction.

I am not afraid of death, but I am terrified of pain. The prospect of being roasted alive was the highest pitch of torment to me. Even Polly looked grave, though her nerves were tougher than the tendons of an ox.

Roasted alive on the prairie…!

The fire sprang towards us like a great flash of lightning. I was amazed at how quickly it advanced. A few more minutes and the two of us would be burnt to a cinder. A few more minutes and...

The torrent of flame was beautiful all the same. It was more beautiful than the sun. I have never seen anything as magnificent. It was so marvellously splendid that I fell to my knees and stretched both hands out towards the fire, laughing like a small child or a fool.

I'll say again that it was as terrible as it was superb, and that it had made me almost crazy. It was too beautiful for human eyes. Only God Himself could have looked straight at the blaze without dying at the sight of it or losing His mind.

But Polly, who has about as much soul as my mules, didn't understand, and looked without really seeing. Nothing surprises her and nothing stirs her admiration.

I hated her for her fearlessness. Oh, how I hated her!... I hate her ferociously because she is stronger and more courageous than I. I hate her, just as a woman abhors the man who overpowers her. I will end up killing her one of these days, purely for the pleasure of defeating her...

'We must not waste any time,' said Polly firmly. Her voice was the same as it always was, not a semitone higher or lower than usual. (Oh, how I hated her for being so calm!) She crouched down and, in the blink of an eye, set fire to the grass in front of her.

I thought for a second that she too had gone mad. And I howled with joy like an Indian taking his revenge.

She wasn't at all disturbed. She was used to my bizarre moods. She despised me too much to be afraid of me.

'Fire fights fire, Jim.'

We drew back. Our fire burned steadily, like a roaring fire on a peaceful hearth. The other fire, fed by the thousands of acres of grass it had devoured, advanced like an oceanic wave of light and noise.

I closed my eyes, drunk on smoke ... When I opened them again two hours later, everything around us was black. It was the ruins of the fire. The inferno had miraculously gone out.

Fire had vanquished fire.

Polly was standing proudly in front of me, hands on hips. What made me furious was that she had not been afraid for a single second.

She will not be any more afraid the day I finally kill her, because she is not scared of death. She is not even scared of God...

She looked at me without batting an eyelid.

'My, aren't you a coward!' she said, scornfully.

PRINCE CHARMING

Narrated by Gesa Karoly

I promised you, my curious little girl, to tell you the true story of Sarolta Andrassy. You knew her, did you not? You remember her black hair with its blue and red highlights, and her lover's eyes, beseeching and melancholy.

Sarolta Andrassy lived in the country with her elderly mother. Her neighbours were the Szechenys, who had just left Budapest once and for all. A bizarre family, in truth! You could have easily mistaken Bela Szecheny for a little girl, and his sister, Terka, for a little boy. Curiously enough, Bela possessed all the feminine virtues and Terka all the masculine faults. Bela's hair was a greenish blonde; Terka's a livelier, more reddish blonde. The brother and sister looked strangely alike – and that is very rare among members of the same family, no matter what they say.

Bela's mother had not yet resigned herself to cutting off the little boy's beautiful blonde curls, or swapping his graceful muslin and velvet skirts for vulgar trousers. She pampered him like a little girl. Meanwhile, Terka continued to grow at will, like a wild weed. She spent all her time outdoors, climbing trees, pilfering fruit and vegetables and stealing from gardens, unbearable and at war with everyone. She was neither tender nor communicative. Bela, on the other hand, was gentleness itself. He showed his adoration for his mother with endless cuddles and caresses. Terka loved no one, and no one loved her.

Sarolta went to visit the Szecheny family one day. Her loving eyes looked out imploringly from her thin, pale face. She liked Bela very much, and they played together for a long time. Terka was cautiously hovering around them. When Sarolta spoke to her, she fled.

She could have been pretty, that incomprehensible Terka... But she was too tall for her age, too thin, too awkward and too ungainly, whereas Bela was so dainty and so sweet!

Several months later, the Szecheny family left Hungary. Sarolta cried bitterly over the loss of her playmate. On the advice of the doctor, his mother had taken him to Nice, along with his recalcitrant little sister. Bela had an extremely sensitive chest, and was in general rather frail.

In her dreams, Sarolta would always conjure up the excessively frail and excessively pretty child whom she could not erase from her memory. And she would say to herself, smiling at the blonde image: 'If I have to get married when I'm older, I would like to marry Bela.'

Several years passed – oh, so slowly, for the impatient Sarolta! Bela must have reached the age of twenty, and Terka seventeen. They were still on the Riviera. And Sarolta grieved through those joyless years, which were illuminated solely by the magic of a dream.

One violet evening, she was dreaming by her window when her mother came to tell her that Bela had returned.

Sarolta's heart sang to the point of bursting. And, the next day, Bela came to see her.

He was the same, and yet somehow even more charming than before. Sarolta was happy that he had retained the gentle, effeminate manner she had so admired. He was still the same fragile child... But that child now possessed an indescribable

34

grace. Sarolta tried in vain to find the reason for the transformation which had made him so attractive. His voice was musical and faraway, like the echo of the mountains. She admired everything about him, even his stone-grey English suit and mauve necktie.

Bela gazed upon the young woman with new eyes, eyes that were strangely beautiful, eyes that were unlike the eyes of other men...

'How thin he is!' observed Sarolta's mother, after he had left. 'Poor thing, he must still be in delicate health.'

Sarolta did not answer. She closed her eyes so she could see Bela once more behind closed eyelids... How handsome, handsome, handsome he was!

He returned the next day, and every day after that. He was the Prince Charming seen only in the pages of children's fairy tales. She could not look him in the eye without feeling faint with passion and yearning. Her expression changed according to the expression of the face she loved. Her heart beat according to the rhythm of that other heart. Unconscious, childlike affection had turned into love.

Bela would turn pale when she came in, diaphanous in her white summer dress. He would sometimes look at her without saying a word, as if he were communing with himself before a perfect statue. Sometimes he would take her hand... His palm was so dry and burning hot that it felt like she was touching the hand of an invalid. A slight fever would then rise to Bela's cheeks.

One day she asked him for news of the undisciplined Terka.

'She is still in Nice,' he answered indifferently. And then they talked about something else. Sarolta realised that Bela did not love his sister at all. Not that it was surprising – she was such a taciturn, savage child!

The inevitable happened. A few months later Bela asked for

her hand in marriage. He had just turned twenty-one. Sarolta's mother had no objections to the union.

It was a fairy-tale betrothal, as delicate as the white roses that Bela brought each day. Their declarations of love were more fervent than poems, and their lips trembled with feeling. The nuptial dream was spent in the deepest silence.

'Why,' Sarolta would ask her fiancé, 'are you worthier of being loved than the other young men? Why do you have a gentleness that they do not? Where did you learn the divine words that they never pronounce?'

The ceremony took place in the greatest privacy. The candles brought out the red highlights in Bela's blonde hair. The incense curled towards him, and the thunder of the organ raised him up and glorified him. For the first time since the world began, the groom was as beautiful as the bride.

They left for the blue shores where the desire of lovers reaches its height. They were seen, a Divine Couple, the eyelashes of one of them grazing the eyelids of the other. They were seen, lovingly and chastely intertwined, her black hair spread over his blonde hair ...

Oh, my curious little girl! This is where the story becomes a little more difficult to relate... Several months later, the real Bela Szecheny appeared. Alas, he was not Prince Charming! He was nothing more than a handsome boy.

He furiously sought to find out who the young imposter was ... And discovered that the imposter was his own sister, Terka.

Sarolta and Prince Charming never went back to Hungary. They are hiding in the depths of a Venetian castle or Florentine mansion. And sometimes you come across them, lovingly and chastely intertwined, a vision of perfect tenderness.

36

THE SISTERS OF SILENCE

I had heard talk, sometimes favourable and sometimes scornful, of a secular monastery born out of one woman's suffering for the suffering of other women. It was, some promised, a fraternal and sacred place in which women's weariness could be assuaged through meditation. Others saw it merely as the unhealthy whim of a woman led astray by grief.

I resolved to see and learn for myself and, one autumn day, I went to the lay convent.

The Superior greeted me with taciturn grace. Everything about her was of a harmonious grey – her hair and dusky eyes, and the melancholy folds of her habit.

'May I ask…?' I began, with embarrassment and awkwardness.

'Do not ask me anything,' interrupted the Grey Lady, not unkindly. 'A question is a brutal violation of the right and duty to be silent. Watch and observe, learn for yourself, but never ask anything of someone as flawed and uncertain as you are.'

And this is what I saw and learned in that strange secular monastery born out of one woman's suffering for the suffering of other women.

The convent was pale in the middle of an immense garden in which only virginal white flowers grew, the flowers of sterility and death. Only the youngest of the recluses were permitted to bestow upon the plants and foliage the delicate care usually given by the gardeners. For according to the law of the convent, the vulgar hand of man should never sully the flowers.

The most mystical of silences reigned throughout the convent.

Those still tormented by the memory of the spoken word would sometimes go to the *parloir*, where they could engage once more, for a few moments, in the vain practice of human speech. Then they would return to the monastic dream with peaceful joy.

The ceremonies of this house of isolation and repose took place by the sad light of the setting sun. Young women with flowing hair murmured verses or intoned chants. A few fervent solitary souls wandered through the galleries, their eyes transfixed by the splendour of the paintings and statues. Others gathered pale flowers from the greenhouses and gardens or lingered to contemplate the infinity of the twilight and sea.

The devout abode was nestled among the rocks like an eagle's nest. Passers-by feared the intensity of its perfumes. The inescapable waft of orange blossom had once caused a virgin to die.

The abyss glimmered blue at the foot of the monastery, more alluring than the Mediterranean Sea. The windows were large and, as they were always wide open onto the sea, encompassed the entire glorious curve of the rainbow. When the organ unleashed its storm of thunder and lightning, when the violins sobbed divine anguish, the eternal steady rhythm of the waves would mingle with their song.

The youngest sister came to me like the incarnation of my most beautiful thought. Her habit was of the same violet as the evening. This woman brought to mind the fragility of mother-of-pearl and the lofty sadness of black swans who leave behind a dark wake. In response to my silence, she murmured:

'I have sought in these shadows not peace, like some exile knocking at the monastery doors. I sought Infinity.'

And I saw that her face resembled the divine face of *Solitude*.

THE CRUELTY OF GEMSTONES

Narrated by Giuseppe Bianchini

In truth, Madonna Gemma, you are aptly named. You are the dazzling, indifferent sister of gemstones ... I love those aquamarines that are the same colour as your eyes. Aquamarines are the most beautiful of all gems: they possess the cold clearness of winter waves.

How you love the jewels that decorate you, oh, my most beautiful Lady! Their dormant life mingles with your breath and your steady heartbeat. Ah, the pearls that hug your voluptuous, cruel neck! Ah, the intensity of those emeralds and the thrill of those opals!

Do you remember why I was once lost for such long months among parchment and crucibles? I wanted to discover the Philosopher's Stone for you. I wanted gold, gold, gold; a stream of gold to pour into your lap. Your body would have bowed under the weight of jewels. The splendour of your necklaces and rings would have put the Dogaressa to shame. The prow of your gondola would have blinded people with its rubies, casting reflections of an autumn sun upon the water ...

How you sparkle in the shadows! ... Turn your beryl eyes away from me. Your implacable soul smiles through your eyes, Madonna.

There are bizarre and awful men who delight in the physical suffering of others. The cries and contortions of the tortured sharpen their weary senses ... You are just like them, you who loathe the ugliness of physical suffering and the barbarism of spilt blood. You take pleasure in rekindling the anguish that lies dormant in people's souls. My words intensify the image of my dread and suffering. That is why you listen with such a bright smile ... You are implacable, Madonna Gemma. But you are so beautiful that I will obey you.

My laborious nights of alchemy forged my strange temperament, which both pleases and displeases you. Ah, those laborious nights! I had a vague feeling that someone was observing my secret studies. You know that as well as I do – perhaps even better. Someone whose invisible gaze was upon me denounced me to the Inquisition. I was accused of black magic. By whom? Perhaps you know, Madonna. Perhaps you know that because of this denunciation, I was locked away seven years ago in a shadowy jail.

How could I possibly describe the horrors of that cell which never saw the dawn? But the most painful torture was in seeing my patient research interrupted just as I was about to discover the Philosopher's Stone. A few hours more and I would have been the master of all the gold and all the gems in the universe.

For a long time, I dreamed with the unbearable persistence of the damned. You would appear to me in a flash of gemstones. I loved you with an inexpressible hatred. You would gesture towards the iron door, the bars on the window and the locks. At night my tortures became even more demonic. Fever and madness carried me away like a sirocco wind ... I sank into an ocean of darkness.

And in order to see you again – do not tremble so, my dazzling Mistress – in order to find you again and expertly torture you with infinite caresses of cruelty, I wanted to escape from my shadowy jail.

On an evening greener than an April river, the jailer entered, making the rusted iron creak. He looked at me with jovial scorn. I had always been as gentle as a nursing mule. I had been as tearfully obedient as a battered child. He asked me whether my fever had subsided at all. I answered by groaning, and I tempered my complaints with professions of gratitude for the interest he was showing me.

He headed for the door after some idiotic words of encouragement. With a furious leap, I seized him from behind and ferociously bit him on the back of the neck. It was such a shock that he fell backwards without letting out even a cry. With one hand I gagged him with straw from my cell. Then I took the bunch of heavy keys which hung from his waist and vigorously beat him.

He took a long time to die, and I lost patience more than once, until I finally saw the river of blood carrying away the fragments of his brains. I was a little disgusted by the hideousness of the sight, but the man was too stupid for me to spend any longer regretting his death. I stripped him and, hiding my bloody clothes under the ample cloak that he habitually wore, I crossed the shadowy corridors.

The hoarse voice of a drunken woman stopped me in my tracks, cold with sweat and trembling more than a Roman with malaria.

'Hurry up, Beppo! The soup is steaming on the table.'

In a moment of realisation such as those sometimes brought on by extreme terror, I realised that the wife of the late jailer was going to give me away.

41

I turned around. In a flash I knew everything I needed to know. First, I noticed that she was abominably drunk. Her breasts were sagging over her stomach, which was swollen as if by pregnancy, like two empty wineskins. Her nose in the semi-darkness resembled a setting sun. On her fat lips the stench of cheap wine was growing increasingly sour. Her hair, clumsily dyed, was red in patches. Great golden rings weighed down her heavy ears, which were more accustomed to the cries of slaughtered animals than to serenades. She was staggering, and from her throat escaped several sour hiccoughs.

What struck me most was the vulgar ostentation of her attire. Her scarlet skirt blazed like a furnace; her bodice, a bellicose yellow, was as loud as the trumpets of victory. Several strands of coral were coiled around her short, fat neck, which would have been so easy to squeeze between murderous hands … Such necks are destined to be strangled, just as certain long, pale, weak things are destined to rape.

A plan, as impromptu as an instinct, sprang to my delirious mind … I kneeled before the enormous peasant woman.

'Madonna,' I sighed, with the grandiloquence of a sentimental fool, 'forgive a too-fervent admirer the cunning that has resulted in the splendid fortune of coming into your presence.'

She studied me, her mouth wide open and her mind addled by tavern wines.

'Fear not, oh redheaded beauty, incarnation of autumn's setting sun! I locked your husband in an empty cell, after knocking him about. I stuffed his mouth with straw, like one of the donkeys he so resembles. Thus silenced, he cannot interrupt our passionate conversation.'

I courageously kissed her kneecaps. Her unsteady eyes widened in astonishment and horror.

I suddenly thought of something. When they arrested me, I had been mounting a delicate ring for you: two sirens, their scales and tangled hair carved out of gold that had turned green, were holding in their cupped arms an aquamarine as beautiful as a drop of glacial sea water. I had managed to hide this gem. I offered it to the creature, whose breasts were shaken by a convulsive tremor.

'I forged this ring for you, oh shining light of my dreams!'

A smile of unconscious bliss widened her heavy drinker's lips.

'Last night, when the first stars set the dead water quivering with illusory life, I hid in the shadows and I sang impassioned *canzoni* for you.'

'I remember,' sighed the drunkard, swooning with pleasure as if a hand had expertly tickled her. 'Oh! Yes, I remember. I heard that beautiful baritone voice climbing so lovingly towards me. But I thought I recognised the accent of the gondolier who has been courting my daughter, Giuseppina, for the past three months.'

'When dawn opened like a rose, I was still under your window, Madonna. I was composing fervent litanies in your honour, as if for the Blessed Virgin ... You are the flame of Venice, the mirage of the setting sun, the smile of tarnished waves ... And in my dreams, I named you Violante.'

'My name is Onesta,' interrupted the dreadful sorceress, complacently stroking her loose breasts.

'I will confess everything to you, Onesta *mia*. I am a great lord whose palace will open its triumphant doors wide for you. Your wandering child's feet will be reflected in marble of an almost diaphanous purity – a wave carrying snow. Listen, Onesta. A dress of silver fabric glistening with pearls will hug the melodious curve of your hips. Aquamarines wedded to moonstones will

43

make you look like starlight on the sea. Two lady's maids will bear the majestic weight of your train, heavy with precious metals and jewels. And two enamoured pages, kneeling before your armchair, will take turns to sing the tender verses that I dictate. I will not offer you flowers, my charming one, for your eyes must not be saddened by the sight of a dying rose. You will look only upon the eternal beauty of opals and emeralds. And into onyx cups I will pour wines as glorious as victories, as sweet as poison and as passionate as kisses …'

Upon hearing mention of wine, my reeling conquest drooled with joy. A light flitted across her wild eyes.

'Wine!' she sighed.

'Let me take you away, Onesta,' I begged. 'Follow me to the palace of love, where the bridal bed is already prepared. I am a magician, and I know of unusual caresses that deviant archangels taught me.'

I paused to savour the effect of my eloquence. Then, knowing that women prefer definite gestures to lavish promises, I leaned towards her. I grazed Onesta's red neck with breath soured by the strict diet of the prison … The encouraging shudders of her Chianti-soaked flesh emboldened me to continue to touch her lightly but expertly, producing fresh hiccoughs. I went on, ingratiating and enticing:

'I will teach you the red-hot peppers of bites … I will teach you the creeping insistence of lips and the tenacious slowness of hands … Your boorish husband has no doubt left you ignorant of such things …' I abruptly dropped all formalities. 'Come along, Onesta! …'

She fixed her stunned eyes on me. 'You do indeed have the words and manners of a great lord,' she stammered, 'but I cannot leave my husband and children for you.'

'Could your husband adorn your feminine splendour as magnificently as I? Would he be able to match precious stones to the colour of your eyes? What is more, you are too graceful to be only a mother, Onesta.'

'Perhaps that is true, after all,' the shrew agreed, fabulously drunk.

'It's as true as truth itself,' I insisted. 'Come, Onesta *mia*.'

The shadows of evening grew darker. A musical softness caused the air to vibrate like the taut strings of a zither.

I suddenly shuddered. We heard resounding steps approaching. My vile companion was on the verge of fainting. I seized her arm violently and ordered her to follow me, as brutally as a carter beating his animal. She obeyed, more passive than an ox.

It was a jailer, whose massive build we could barely make out in the hazy twilit corridor. I shivered feverishly when he called, 'Are you going to take in the evening air on the canal?'

'My husband is a little unwell, Jacopo,' muttered Onesta. 'We are both going to have a rest. Good night.'

'Good night,' said the man, who continued on his way, humming as he did so.

We arrived at the large doorway. The guard, in response to Onesta's choked request, opened the gate and let us out into the blue half-light …

The southerly wind was carrying aromatic memories and I know not what evil pleasures. The lagoon was as tepid and grotesque as a bared sex. I absent-mindedly caressed Onesta's breasts.

'Here is a gondola, my pensive beauty. Deign to follow me to the palace of my amorous dreams.'

She embarked, sunk in a happy stupor … I am as good at

45

steering a boat as I am at torturing a woman, Gemma. I took the place of the slightly dumbfounded gondolier, reassuring the good fellow by slipping him one of the few gold coins that had escaped the rapacity of the jailers.

We let ourselves be swept along the spellbinding canal. Oh, the cruelty of the waters and the night! Red and yellow lights from a dwelling with its doors wide open fell upon the waves. The music of mandolins and raspy guitars floated towards us from a public house, the haunt of sailors and gondoliers.

'Come, my immortal Lady ... There is Asti Spumante in the private rooms ...'

We entered. The stench of foul garlic and bad wine suffocated me as soon as I crossed the threshold. I drew the curtains on our imminent pleasures. Onesta was already dozing off into a drunken stupor.

I thought about her awakening. When the drink was no longer fermenting in her empty head, what terrors would cause her stupid eyes to widen? She would denounce me ... And if I abandoned her immediately, relying on her drowsiness, I feared that she might return to her senses.

But why not admit it? I was filled with the cruelty of the waters and the night. Mortal lust had made me like a wild beast gone mad. I threw myself upon the abominable drunkard, and I made use of her with a frenzy that even your most sophisticated kisses, Gemma, have never inspired in me. I sobbed quietly at the overwhelming pleasure, like a sorrowful child. And I bit those despicable lips until they bruised.

But a stronger desire took hold of me. I took advantage of the stupor into which my companion, overcome by the intensity of the spasms, was sinking, and, grasping her firmly by the throat, I took great delight in strangling her ... Some short, fat necks are destined to be strangled ...

Onesta's death throes were brief – too brief, even. Full of wine and weakened by sexual convulsions, she quickly succumbed between my powerful hands ... I am as good at strangling as I am at caressing.

Her corpse was so ridiculously hideous that I began to laugh. My carnal desires relieved, I became very gentle. The male in me was satisfied. A victim had been sacrificed to the cruelty of the waters and the night. I departed, my soul at peace.

'Why are you leaving your companion here?' asked a barmaid who was being fondled by a sailor.

'She is too drunk to stand. She is sleeping as deeply as the dead in their coffins.' And I smiled innocently at this joke, whose delicate humour only I could appreciate.

The waters and the night approved of me and took me in with indulgent gentleness. I spat upon the reflections of the stars and I sang my most beautiful songs to the sea.

An hour went by, light and diaphanous. The reflections of the stars died at the bottom of the lagoon. Then the dawn broke, strident and triumphant as a clarion call. I rounded the Dogana Cape and followed the Giudecca Canal. The rocking motion of the gondola gave rhythm to my peaceful dreams. The green water had the treacherous languor of your sleepy eyes, Madonna ...

The gondola came to a stop outside your door. Although it was daylight, your house was slumbering in the shadows of sleep. The smell of indolence and lingering dreams rose towards me. I made my way to your room.

You were sleeping. Your marble face made my blood run cold. I trembled at the sight of your motionless eyelids. Your brow was mottled by the darkness, making it look just like the blueish brows of the deceased.

I came towards you, hands clasped. I shivered, my entire body frozen to the marrow. Slowly, slowly, you opened your eyes, Gemma *mia*. And I saw in your wild eyes so monstrous a terror that *I understood* ... I knew whose invisible gaze had long ago hidden in the shadows while I worked among my crucibles and parchment. I knew which hand had scrawled those treacherous lines denouncing me to the Inquisition ... I knew who had betrayed me, out of an inclination for evil ...

And it is since that day that you have loved me, Gemma *mia*. You love me with all your terror. Horror alone can make your weary body and soul quiver with life. And because you fear me, you love me. You know that I will one day break you, whenever the fancy strikes. You know that I will destroy you the moment you stop pleasing me. Silent with passive horror, you closely watch my movements and my steps ... You await the end. But the moment has not yet arrived, for your body still tempts me like the fragrant juice of watermelon and the flesh of ripe figs. Madonna Gemma, your hour has not yet come ...

I want your lips ... Kisses, kisses, kisses.

FOREST BETRAYAL

Narrated by Blue Dirk

I am not a wicked man, even though they call me the Forest Devil. They call me Blue Dirk too, because I have tattoos all over my body. Joan was also blue with tattoos. Joan was my wife. We were not married according to the Anglican Church, as there were no clergymen where we met, but she was my wife nonetheless.

She had the most beautiful tattoos a woman could ever desire. There was no American Indian woman more artfully adorned with tomahawks and turtles. I had drawn a devil with buffalo horns and a cow's tail for her right leg. A serpent circled her right wrist like a bracelet. And above her left breast were two hearts pierced by a single arrow, with our initials intertwined.

I have no idea why they called me the Forest Devil. It is true that I'm a little nasty when I've had too much to drink. I killed a couple of men without realising it when I was drunk, and I even knocked out two or three women who resisted me when I tried to do them violence – the eau de vie made me amorous. But I would never have done anything like that had I not been under the influence. It is also true that I took a little girl by force, but that was because I had been wandering alone for a whole month without seeing even one woman, no matter how old or ugly. I assure you that I would never have behaved in such a fashion had I not been so terribly deprived. It was only a little bit of pleasure.

And anyway, the child screamed so loudly! I left, after rewarding her with a good slap. I don't like screaming. Children should never make a sound. I did burn the feet of an old farmer's wife when she wouldn't tell me where she'd hidden her money. But since she ended up telling me where she'd hidden her booty, I didn't do her any more harm. I am an excellent fellow, at heart. Besides, the smell of charred flesh was too hard to bear. In short, none of that is very important, and I do not know why they call me the Forest Devil.

What is murder, anyway? It merely brings the inevitable end a few years closer. Is twenty minutes of torture really so terrible? Is it not a thousand times less hideous than years of agony? ... Cancer, for example ... Personally, I would much rather be killed than die of cancer ... If I have ever seen off somebody who would have otherwise been immortal, I would of course have a great weight on my conscience.

In the case of the little girl, I only anticipated the natural violence that, in all probability, some other man would have perpetrated on her body. I have never possessed a pubescent virgin, but they tell me that the first time is always very painful for a woman. And so the little girl would have soon discovered the brutality of men.

It is true that a great number of women die virgins. Even so, I have heard it said that this is not a normal fate for a woman. It seems to be almost immoral, even. The people who told me this are what you would call 'healthy-minded'. Being healthy-minded means thinking like everyone else.

I was perhaps wrong in roasting the feet of the old farmer's wife. But why was she so miserly? If I succeeded in curing her of her stinginess, then I rendered her a great service. Perhaps I've facilitated her entry into the Kingdom of Heaven.

I am a sterling character, at heart. I am going to give you proof of it. When the residents of a little Hindu village ravaged by two tigers came to me for help, I immediately went to their aid. In truth, they did offer me a handsome reward for ridding them of those damned beasts. Yet I assure you that love of my neighbour was the determining reason for my kind undertaking.

Joan was with me ... An admirable hunting companion ... That is exactly why I kept her so long.

One of the few villagers who had escaped the claws of the tiger and tigress showed us the beasts' favourite hideout. We tied a white calf to a nearby tree and, the following day, Joan and I began our adventure.

We took the *kullal*[2] with us, who doubled as both guide and water bearer, bright-eyed Mangkali, my head *shikari*[3] and Sala and Nursoo, two slightly younger beaters.

We had trekked several miles when we heard the tiger's magnificent roar. Joan shuddered, almost sensually. Her eyes widened with enthusiasm and pride. We were to confront an adversary worthy of us.

'*Wuh hai!*' wailed the *kullal*, whose every bronze-coloured limb was trembling, 'that is the *sahib* of my village ... that is, the king of the land.'

His abject terror was rising by the minute. Sensing that he was about to do something mad, Joan told him with her habitual calm:

'If you try to run away, the tiger will certainly get you, old boy. I advise you to stay behind us: that is your only chance of surviving.'

Mangkali and Joan led the way. Joan had the eyes of a lynx. We reached some rocks, from which point we could see the sacrificial calf.

'Look,' whispered Joan.

I looked. In the dusk I could see only a white, immobile mass.

'The calf is dead,' observed Mangkali, very quietly.

Joan simply waved her forefinger in the air.

'*Doom hilta hai*,'[4] agreed Nursoo, the youngest *shikari*. He had understood my wife's mime.

'Can you see the tiger?' I asked Joan.

She indicated that she could. Straining my eyes, I made out the shape of the animal. Ah! The superb beast!

Joan quickly set off. I followed her. The tiger was so busy devouring the unfortunate white calf alive that he did not hear us coming. We took cover behind a tree, twenty yards from the tiger. The calf's neck was disappearing into the maw of the beautiful monster, whose paws were cruelly tearing at his victim.

'Don't take aim yet,' Joan advised. 'We must not wound him without killing him.'

The calf put up a struggle, with supreme effort. His adversary's attempts to regain his hold exposed the pale target that was the tiger's belly and chest. He had turned onto his left side. I aimed for his heart and, somewhat anxiously, I fired.

With one magnificent leap, he rolled over, jaws open, breath coming in gasps. Joan approached the dying animal and, with a blow of her rifle butt, broke his spine, putting him out of his misery. The *kullal*'s teeth were chattering. Joan, irritated beyond all measure by his quivering cowardice, grabbed him impatiently by the arm.

'Come and see him up close,' she said, pointing to the dead tiger. 'He is a beautiful beast.'

But the terrified *kullal* only emitted moans of terror. Joan pursed her lips in an expression of inexpressible contempt.

'My friend,' she said to me, putting her rough killer's hand on my shoulder, 'our work is not yet over. The tigress will come back to join the tiger.'

'You are right, Joan.'

She did not take her heavy hand off my shoulder. For the first time in my life, I saw her hesitate, darkening at the prospect of the task ahead.

'It will not be easy,' she said, very slowly. 'Perhaps it is stupid, but I have a feeling that she will give us trouble. Tigresses are much more fearsome than tigers, Dirk. They are more ferocious and more treacherous.'

'Are you trying to teach me how to do my job? Come on, surely you're not afraid. It would be the first time. But if you don't want to go on with this …'

'You know perfectly well, idiot, that I am not afraid of death. Since we all have to go one way or another, it is better to go in the open air, young and strong, than gradually rot in a sick room that suffocates you and smells foul. As for drugs – ugh! But I still have a feeling the tigress will give us trouble.'

She gazed at the calm and beautiful forest. The branches of the trees were like motionless pythons. The creepers were coiled like green serpents. Whispers of danger and betrayal were rising up from the ground and falling from the leaves. The stars were all out, like flaming flowers.

'How beautiful it all is!' It was the first time Joan had expressed such a feeling. She was usually as resistant to wonder as she was to surprise and terror. Emotion offended her. She considered it a sign of weakness. 'It is beautiful, very beautiful. And it makes me think of things I have never worried about before. Dirk, is there anything beyond death?'

I grumbled unhappily. I don't much like talking about things I know nothing about.

'Do you believe the clergyman was right when he said that there is another self, and that this second person does not die at the same time as the first?'

'You're annoying me, Joan.'

'Too bad. I have to talk to someone this evening. I know that you will not understand me.' She stopped, with a faraway look. 'It is not that I am afraid. Oh, no! But I do wonder why I don't know such a simple thing. And I also wonder why nobody in the whole world, neither the soberest clergyman nor the best doctor, has ever known such a simple thing. And yet it is, in fact, the only thing of any importance. How do you think that happened, Dirk?'

'How should I know?'

'Naturally, you do not know. You are not intelligent, but even if you were, it would make no difference. Dirk, we have hunted together for fifteen years. We have slept side by side. We have ended up resembling one another, just as our souls resemble one another's. No matter how well you lie to me, you will never succeed in taking me in. I understand you. You are not a wicked man and I am not a wicked woman. Oh, of course we both have a few things on our consciences. You in particular. As for me, I have only one thing to my credit – I have been a loyal and devoted hunting companion. Women are good, in general. But I am not good, Dirk, because I am too much like a man.'

'You are talking as if you were going to die, Joan. You are annoying and stupid.'

'It is strange to see how alone one is when one is going to die ... One must be very cold ... I had never worried about any of this before this evening. One must be frightfully alone when one goes to the Beyond! Do you think you meet anyone along the road, other souls who departed at the same time as you?'

'Shut up, will you?'

'And then, one must be so naked. No flesh, no bones. A mass with neither form nor contour. One must float, like a cloud. It must be extremely disagreeable. And one no longer has a name. One is no longer Joan, killer of tigers and wife of the Forest Devil. One is not even someone. One is something. One wanders unknowingly, just like that. One desires to be someone, to become someone again, to be called by a name, to assume a body. One is very alone and very naked and very cold.'

'Will you ever shut up?'

'Yes, I will shut up, because I have said everything I had to say.'

We went back to the campsite. Joan, who had gone to fetch water to boil the kettle, did not return. Some time passed.

I would have heard her cry out if she had been attacked by the tigress, I thought. *Oh, that bitch. Is she cheating on me with a Hindu?* Then I thought that it was hardly probable. Joan was not a sensual woman, and she despised the natives.

We went out looking for her, taking the road which led to the river. All of a sudden, the *shikari*, Nursoo, shouted three times: 'The tigress! The tigress! The tigress!'

And I heard the horrible caterwauling of the beast and the crunching of bone between her jaws.

There was nothing we could do. We had got there too late. I realised what had happened. The tigress, lying in wait, had pounced upon Joan and, sinking her claws into her breast, she must have bitten her on the lips, which had prevented her from crying out for help ... Tigresses are as cunning as they are cruel, you know ...

So my poor Joan was eaten up. I lamented her for a long time, because she was an excellent hunting companion. I am neither soft nor a coward, but for the rest of my days I will hear that caterwauling, at once furious and satisfied, and the crunching of bone between frightful jaws.

PARADOXICAL CHASTITY

I was brought to Genoa by sheer chance. The trip there, though difficult and slow, had in no way diminished my strength and courage, and I had been in the city for three days. I need not spell it out: 'Man is nothing but a dog in heat,' a wise man once said ... In short, the lonely nights were getting on my nerves. I resolved to find a mistress for an hour or so.

One of my friends, to whom I had confided my problem, offered to take me to the house of the procuress Myriam, famous for her knack for arranging love affairs. Machiavelli himself would have admired her in secret. She had the best choice of women and a superb understanding of her art.

Her palazzo was reputed to have fairy-tale magnificence. I followed my friend to the house of the procuress, and I saw at once that my friend had not exaggerated its splendour. We climbed a staircase of the purest white marble, like a glacier. The engravings on the bronze banister depicted trembling hamadryads leaning over rivers and fountains to listen to the whispers of the naiads. Solemn statues illuminated the half-shadows with their polished reflections.

Two Moorish servants preceded me into a vast room draped with hangings of deep-red velvet. I observed the carvings on the majestic fireplace. Motionless Vestal Virgins watched over the hearth. The light fell upon a painting in which two huntresses were bringing an offering from their triumphant bows to an image of Artemis.

The soft shades of the carpet evoked an entire lost Persia. The vases of pottery, earthenware and wrought metal were miracles of workmanship. They were worthy of flowers. A flamboyant summer of roses was wasting away in its own perfume. The immense bay window looked out onto the sea, which shimmered beneath our bedazzled eyes, streaming with molten silver and sprinkled with crystal.

A woman entered. Never had I seen beauty more bountiful. She glowed with the exotic magnificence of beautiful Jewish women. I gazed upon the red and blue highlights of her black hair, pale with ecstasy. Her eyes were the colour of black grapes. The red velvet of the curtains and tapestries framed her with their bright flames, and intensified the dull warmth of her flesh of amber and nard. Her mouth had the fresh redness of watermelon.

The woman was a living splendour. She resembled the garden of a queen, a priceless jewel, a piece of fabric beautifully embroidered by patient hands. There was something serious and distant about her that inspired, or, rather, imposed respect.

My friend bowed in deference. 'Myriam, allow me to present one of my friends,' he said.

I stood there, astounded. This creature, more beautiful than the most beautiful courtesan, was the procuress!

She smiled. Jezebel in her gold and gemstones must have smiled in the same immodest and majestic fashion. 'You will be dazzled, signor,' she promised, as she disappeared behind the red cloud of the curtains.

My companion looked at me with curiosity.

'But she is the one I want!' I cried, wild with wonder and amazement.

He shrugged his shoulders. 'Beware of turning your lusting

eyes towards her,' he advised. 'She is as unattainable as a snowy and icy mountain top.'

'I did not know about this jesting humour of yours, my good man.'

'But I am not joking. Myriam is chaste. She is reputed to be a virgin. She traffics in the virtue of others, but keeps her own intact. She knows the value of what others sell or give away too lightly. And besides, her occupation must have inspired in her a horror, or disgust, of men. I will say it again: get the thought out of your mind.'

Shrugging off his idiotic remark, I let out a cry of impatience … At that moment, the doors opened wide and a bevy of young women as rosy as the Graces entered in a buzzing horde. The air filled with fragrance. But I had eyes only for Myriam, the black sun among the stars. Never had I so deeply and so intensely understood, felt and loved the noble attraction of dark-haired women.

'Allow me to present Myrtô the Sicilian,' said Myriam. 'Her flesh has the scent of ripe apples. This is Violante, a flower of Spain. She is as lovely as her name. And this is Lollia, who plays the guitar as skilfully as a Venetian, and Néis, who dances like a faun. This is Néméa, as blonde as gold in the sun.'

'I adore blondes,' stated my friend. 'And this one is as light as one could wish for. What foamy whiteness!' He followed Néméa, who led him away.

Noticing my lack of enthusiasm for her female entourage, Myriam whispered in my ear: 'If you long for someone of high ranking, I will introduce you to a marchioness of heroic lineage. But before removing her mask, she demands that you swear to the Holy Virgin that you will never utter a word about it. She is beautiful but poor.'

I refused with a gesture.

'I know what you are thinking. You are in love, but the woman is stubborn. Whisper to me, handsome gentleman, the name of this indifferent woman. No one is as talented as I at words that ingratiate and persuade. Even if she is cold as a statue, I will bring her to you in a few days. And, if she persists in her stony, snowy frigidity, I will find you a young woman just like her, who resembles her feature for feature but is gentler and more submissive to your desires.'

I stared at her. She had put her hand on my arm, but her cool touch burned me. Myriam's voice had become even more amenable. 'I would like to speak with you alone,' I interrupted abruptly.

Every part of her brown face smiled. 'Go, my doves.' The gracious forms vanished.

From my finger I removed a very rare ruby, as beautiful as the blood of a wounded woman, and I threw it, along with my heavy purse, on the onyx table. 'Take them, Myriam, and take this Mediterranean-blue sapphire too. In exchange, you will give me your most expert kisses.'

She smiled again, but with a sharper smile. 'You are mistaken, sir,' she replied, very calmly. 'I am the merchant, not the merchandise.'

I met her haughty eye. 'You are a first-rate coquette,' I laughed nervously. 'But you please me. I will pour all the gold you ask for into the palms of your hands.'

'I sell the other girls, not myself.'

I pulled her against me, mad with desire. 'Love me, for I love you.' And I pressed my feverish kiss upon her cold lips.

She stepped back and, tearing herself away from my embrace,

slapped me so violently that I staggered. 'Get out,' she ordered.

But my male vanity protested, and I resolved to force this woman to submit to my wishes. I went over to her, my senses so inflamed that I was ready to rape. My hand reached for her timid breasts, impetuously lifted by an angry intake of breath.

Swifter than the flight of a sparrow, she seized a dagger, a marvel of niello and precious stones that hung decoratively from her belt, and plunged it into my chest. I fell. A sharp pain pierced my heart ... I sank into the depths of a red night.

The most skilful doctors only just managed to wrest me from the tenacious claws of death. I was cured by some miracle of vigorous youth.

Never again did I cross the threshold of the procuress, that strange woman who was perverse and pure, immodest and unattainable.

THE SPLENDID PROSTITUTE

An account narrated by an Envious Man

And Glory appeared to me. I could make out her eyes, which were the colour of copper, and of her hair, which was the colour of blood. I was a little surprised by her appearing, for I had hardly hoped to take advantage of her fickle favours. But Glory is a woman – that is, cruel and perverse – and she loves to flaunt her star-sequined skirt before those she despises.

I braced myself, so I could gaze upon her not with love, but with all my pride and all my contempt. And I said, slowly:

'My house is not some hovel with vials of cheap perfume and pots of make-up lying around. What are you doing in this empty bedroom, furnished only with memories? Why do you seek to enchant a has-been like me? ... I see you for what you are. I have turned my back on you in disgust. You are the drunken mistress of thieves and charlatans. You enjoy the stench of slaughterhouses and you inhale the precious fumes of blood with delight. You are as blind as those who make a profession of judging their neighbours. You are as stupid as a warrior and as corrupt as a whore. You would rather abandon yourself to those who rape you, and, if you happen to excite a proud woman or a poor man, it is only the passing fancy of a drunk courtesan. Your sex is public property, and I, for one, would not care to welcome such an ugly whore into my modest bed.'

'You are lying, just like a child,' she answered. 'I haven't the slightest intention of abandoning myself to you ... Besides, you know you would shed blood for my mercenary kiss. The foolish vanity of being talked about! But it possesses you just as much as anyone else.'

'On the other hand,' I interrupted, 'the pathetic joy of creating legends about oneself in which malice is equalled only by foolishness! Oh, the poisoned words that creep into your veins and flow in your blood! ... You are even more of a slanderer than a cowardly denouncer of secret sins. You are the one who privately dishonours all those you publicly exalt.'

'Perhaps you are right. But there are good, sentimental people who hope, by their writings and their works, to attract towards their solitude the kindred spirits of today and of tomorrow.'

'They are only kindred spirits as long as they remain undiscovered,' I objected. 'I have not met one person on earth whom I did not later regret having understood too well and known too long.'

'You are still lying, for I have seen a woman by your side, whose indulgent sweetness made you weep with love.'

'This time, you are right. He who has met a loyal woman along his path need no longer seek or desire anything else. But what do my life and my thoughts matter to you, the battered servant of butchers and public speakers? You who engrave the insignificant names of kings in marble, and scorn the obscure names of good poets? You who place Hugo, the prince of the bourgeoisie, above Rimbaud and Charles Cros?[5] And finally, you who allowed the sacred songs of Myrtis of Anthedon, Telesilla the heroine and in particular, the melodious, virginal Erinna of Telos to perish? Even your servants have unspoken contempt of your caresses. They return to their manuscripts or canvases with disgust, just as the dog in scripture returns to his vomit. Like opium smokers and drunkards, they are damned by an incurable vice. Indeed. Go away … Night is falling, as beautiful as impending death. And the hope of a short and painless death is a comfort to those who sit in the shadows.'

THE SAURIENNE

Narrated by Mike Watts

The sun is terrible. The sun is more terrible than plague and wild animals and gigantic black snakes. It is more terrible than fever. It is a thousand times more terrible than death.

The sun scorched the back of my neck and my temples and my skull; it dried and bleached my hair like grass in a heatwave. Anyone else would have gone mad after those long treks through the desert. At times it seemed to me that molten lead was streaming down my forehead and along my limbs. Oh! Oh! Anyone else would have gone mad, but I have a good strong head and body. I have seen people howling and waving their arms like demons after long days of trekking through the desert. The sun, beating down on their stupid brains, had given them strange ideas. But not me – I have always been calm and reasonable.

The sun is terrible.

Towards the end of an afternoon on which the sun's long, sharp rays were still coming down like javelins, I came across a very strange woman. I am no coward, but this woman scared me because of her horrifying likeness to a crocodile.

Do not think for a moment that I am mad. I've got all my wits; I even have quite a solid reputation for having common sense. I assure you that this woman looked like a crocodile.

She had rough, scaly skin. Her little eyes terrified me. Her enormous mouth terrified me even more, with its sharp, enormous teeth. I swear, this woman looked like a crocodile.

She was looking at the water when I got up the courage to approach her.

'What are you looking at there?' I asked her, at once curious and secretly appalled.

She fixed her terrible little reptilian eyes on mine. I instinctively drew back.

'I am looking at the crocodiles,' she answered. 'I am somewhat akin to them. I know all their habits. I call them by their names. And they recognise me when I walk along the river.'

She spoke in such a simple, natural tone of voice that I shuddered with an icy terror. I knew that *she was telling the truth.* I didn't dare stare at her rough, scaly skin.

'The king and the queen of the crocodiles are my close friends,' she continued. 'The king lives at Denderah. The queen, who is just as powerful as he and even more cruel, preferred to go forty leagues higher, so she could reign by herself. She wants undivided power. He loves his independence too, and so they live separately, while remaining very good friends. They meet only occasionally, in order to make love.'

I saw in her eyes a gleam of ferocious lust, which made my teeth chatter. I use that banal expression on purpose, for at that moment I understood it in all its strength and horror. The frightful sun was oppressing me and crushing me with the weight of a giant. Its liquid fire scorched me. And yet my teeth were knocking together as though it were winter, when the freezing cold numbs your blood.

'I believe you,' I gasped.

She came closer to me, with an awkward motion that was heavily suggestive … The monster's simpering was more terrifying than her deformity.

'No, you don't believe me. What is your name?'

'Mike Watts.'

'All right, Mike, I swear to you that I can ride crocodiles. Do you believe me?'

I was sweating even more profusely than I had been, but this time it was a cold sweat that froze my limbs. 'Yes, I believe you.'

And I did believe her, in fact. I am not crazy. I have never been crazy, even in the desert, even when I was thirsty. But I did believe her, and you would have believed her, just as I did.

She smirked obnoxiously – which is to say, she opened her mouth. She opened her abominable caiman's mouth very wide and she silently showed me all her teeth. A shiver rippled over her whole body, and there it all was … Oh, God who invented hell!

'No, you don't believe me,' the Saurienne repeated. 'But I am going to prove that I am telling the truth.' She inspected the yellowish river, heavy with sand and silt. 'There's one,' she said, very quietly. 'Step back.'

I did not wait for her to repeat her command. I ran off as fast as I could. But I stopped a short distance from the river, suddenly bound by something even more compelling than terror itself.

Just as the crocodile was opening its jaws, I saw her pull herself up onto its back, and, for the duration of a nightmare, I saw her riding an alligator[6] …

I am not raving. I am in my right mind. I am not lying, either. Lying is all right for civilised men. The rest of us never lie. We cannot stand the complications.

The Saurienne came back towards me, leaving the crocodile to writhe heavily in the brackish water. She came back, her eyes gleaming with triumph … and with something else …

She waited for some expression of surprise and approval ... But I was staggering like a drunk, and I could only mumble incoherent syllables – *buh*, *buh*, *buh*. And I was drooling like an idiot.

She looked at me with the fierce, lustful eyes of a monster in heat. 'Come here,' she ordered.

I tried to follow her. I could not do it. I made the choked gestures of a madman in a straitjacket.

A few steps from where we were standing was a tangle of very tall grass, and trees with branches like giant snakes. She was looking at this shelter out of the corner of her eye ... I had no trouble figuring out what she wanted from me ...

It would be difficult for me to explain what I was experiencing at that moment. All sorts of ideas were racing through my brain, like a pack of mad dogs. I knew I had to kill the monster, but how ... How? Bullets or blades would bounce off her shell without doing her any harm. Now, did she not have some weak spot? No ... But yes ... Her eyes ... HER EYES!

A fevered, delirious joy took hold of me, a joy known only to the shipwrecked as they step on land once more, or to the sick who at last see the dawn dispel a night of horrible hallucinations. I danced; I managed to swallow my saliva; I even stammered a few stupid words of love.

I emptied my flask in one gulp. The thought of my impending deliverance ran through my veins, along with the benevolent warmth of the brandy ... I now had the strength to perform the necessary murder ... And, while the Saurienne was awaiting carnal satisfaction, with her eyes rolled back in her drunken head, I took out my knife. I took out my knife, went over to the monster sprawled on the grass, and I carved out her eyes ...

I carved out her eyes, I tell you. Oh, I am courageous, me! You can say all sorts of malicious things about me, but you can never make out that I am a coward. Lots of men in my predicament would have lost their heads. But I did not hesitate for a second ...

And, as I was going away from there, I turned round to see the yellowish river, heavy with sand and silt, one last time.

THE VEIL OF VASHTI

Innocent as Christ, who died for men, she has
devoted herself to women.
(Flaubert, *The Temptation of Saint Anthony*)

Queen Vashti prepared a feast for the women in the house of King Ahasuerus.

The palace courtyard sparkled like the setting sun. The pavement of mother-of-pearl and black stones was bloody with roses. The columns of marble were decorated with garlands of daturas. Green, blue and white curtains quivered above the golden beds, held up by silver rings and strands of byssus.

The feast lasted seven days. The slaves poured drinks into malachite vessels, each one with different engravings, and there was an abundance of royal wine.

On the seventh day, Vashti, who was surrounded by the princesses of Persia and Media and by the wives of the noblemen and the provincial leaders, was listening to the female musicians. They sang of the power and the wisdom of the queens of India, who have sea-green serpents for lovers.

Vashti's face was as beautiful as the night. Her proud eyebrows arched triumphantly. Her eyelids were lowered, as solemn as the violet eyelids of sleep. And her black eyes, in which all of Ethiopia shone, were vast, unknown countries.

The musicians stopped playing. An old Jewish slave woman recounted the legend of Iblis and of a certain Lilith, who was created before Eve and was the First Woman.

' ... And Lilith, scornful of the love of man, preferred the embrace of the Serpent. That is why Lilith has been punished for centuries. Some have seen her in the melancholy moonlight, weeping over dead serpents. She is like the supernatural dreams of the solitary. She plagues innocent sleepers with dreams. She is Fever, she is Desire, she is Perversity. In truth, Lilith has been punished for centuries because nothing will ever satisfy her hunger for the Absolute.'

'I would have been like Lilith,' Queen Vashti mused out loud.

'Iblis, like his mortal companion, is cursed, O Sovereign. Iblis is the fallen star who sinks into the darkness, because he dreamed of being God's equal.'

'I would have been like Iblis,' Queen Vashti mused out loud.

'Iblis is the foremost of the vanquished, O Sovereign ... Because Iblis desired the impossible.'

'I love the vanquished,' whispered Vashti. 'I love all those who attempt the impossible.'

The old Jewish woman, who had the wisdom of the ages, seemed to be gathering her thoughts. Vashti tore a pink lotus into shreds.

A roar of laughter shook the marble columns and caused the mother-of-pearl and the porphyry of the pavement to tremble. It was the courtiers, intoxicated by the magnificence of the king. The king, his heart gladdened by the wine, was encouraging them.

Vashti lowered her eyelids to conceal the contempt in the depths of her Ethiopian eyes. Her skin was emitting the spices and the myrrh oil and the perfumes used by the women.

The green, white and blue curtains parted ... Vashti covered her face with a grey veil encrusted with beryls that resembled dusk by the sea.

The seven eunuchs who served King Ahasuerus entered, their footsteps silent. The princesses of Persia and Media stopped their whispering and murmuring … The eunuchs kneeled at the feet of Queen Vashti and informed her of King Ahasuerus's order. Vashti gazed at them through her grey veil, her eyes like the bored eyes of lions.

In the silence that followed the words of the messengers, one could have heard a rose shedding its petals.

Vashti rose from her golden bed and spoke, erect and majestic:

'O princesses of Persia and Media, King Ahasuerus has ordered Mehuman, Biztha, Harbona, Bigtha, Abagtha, Zethar and Carcas, the seven eunuchs who serve King Ahasuerus, to bring Queen Vashti to him, her royal crown upon her head, in order to present her beauty to the people and to the nobility.'

There was a tense silence. In truth, King Ahasuerus's order had no precedent in the history of the Persians, nor of the Medians, nor in the history of India, nor in the history of the Ethiopians, for the impure gaze of man must never profane the mystery of the female face.

Vashti continued, very slowly: 'Here is Queen Vashti's answer to King Ahasuerus: *When Queen Vashti received King Ahasuerus's order from the eunuchs, Queen Vashti refused to go.*'

The eunuchs withdrew. Everybody's face had changed. A Persian princess dropped the cup from which she had been drinking, and the king's wine spread all over the porphyry and mother-of-pearl pavement … The king's wine spread, red as a pool of blood.

The old Jewish woman tore her robe and beat her chest: 'Woe betide you and all of us, O Queen!'

Rigid as a marble statue with black stones for eyes, Vashti

spoke thus to the princesses of Persia and Media: 'I will never unveil my sacred face before a crowd of drunken courtiers. The impure gaze of man must never profane the mystery of my face. King Ahasuerus's order is an insult to my pride as a woman and as a queen.'

The old Jewish woman, seizing an incense-burner, covered her white head with ashes and wailed: 'Rebellion is a deadly thing, O Queen! Think about the rebellion of Iblis. Think about the rebellion of Lilith. Think about the eternal punishment of Lilith and of Iblis!'

'What does it matter!' said Queen Vashti then. And she pronounced these solemn words: 'It was not only King Ahasuerus that I was thinking about when I acted … For my actions will reach all women, and they will say: *King Ahasuerus ordered for Queen Vashti to be brought to him, and she did not go.* And from this day onwards, the princesses of Persia and Media will know that they are no longer the servants of their husbands, and that man is no longer the master of his house, but that woman is free and a mistress who is equal to the master in his house.'

The princesses of Persia and Media rose and looked at one another with new eyes that shone with the pride of being liberated.

The old Jewish woman was still wailing …

The green, white and blue curtains parted a second time, and the seven eunuchs of King Ahasuerus reappeared. The seven eunuchs, Mehuman, Biztha, Harbona, Bigtha, Abagtha, Zethar and Carcas, spoke thus to Queen Vashti:

'O Queen, when the king heard Queen Vashti's answer to King Ahasuerus, the king was very irritated; in fact, he was burning with rage. Then the king went to speak to the sages who have the wisdom of the ages. He had with him Carschena, Schethar, Admatha, Tarsis, Meres, Marsena, Memucan, seven princes of Persia and Media, who are in the king's inner circle and who are the foremost men in his kingdom. "What law," said he, "should apply to Queen Vashti for not having carried out what King Ahasuerus ordered through his eunuchs?"

'Memucan addressed the king and the princes: "It is not only with regard to the king that the queen has behaved badly, it is also towards all the princes and all men in all the provinces of King Ahasuerus. This is because the queen's actions will come to be known by all the wives and will lead them to scorn their husbands. They will say: *King Ahasuerus ordered for Queen Vashti to be brought to him, and she did not go*. And from this day onwards, the princesses of Persia and Media who have learned of the queen's actions will relate it to all the king's chiefs; much contempt and anger will result from that. If the king feels it right, let us publish on his behalf, and let us inscribe among the laws of the Persians and the Medes – with infringement prohibited – a royal order according to which Vashti will never again appear before King Ahasuerus, and the king will give the title of queen to another who is better than she. The edict of the king will be known throughout the kingdom, no matter how large, and all the women will honour their husbands, from the noblest to the humblest."

'The king and the princes judged in favour of this opinion.'

The princesses of Media and Persia wept silently.

Vashti stood up, and, with a haughty gesture, removed the royal crown from her hair. She also removed the pearls from her neck, the pale sapphires from her fingers, the beryls from her arms and the emeralds from her waist. She took off her purple

74

sea silk gown and put on the torn tunic that belonged to the old Jewish woman. Then she placed a crown of pink lotuses upon her head and wrapped her entire body in her dusky veil.

'Where are you going, Mistress?' sobbed the old Jewish woman, who was bowing down before her.

'I am going towards the desert, where human beings are as free as lions.'

'No man has ever returned from the desert, Mistress, and never has a woman ventured there.'

'Perhaps I will perish there of hunger. Perhaps I will perish there between the teeth of wild animals. Perhaps I will perish there of loneliness. But since the rebellion of Lilith, I am the first free woman. My actions will come to be known by all women, and all those who are slaves in the houses of their husbands or fathers will secretly envy me. They will think of my glorious rebellion and say: "Vashti spurned being queen in order to be free."'

And Vashti set out for the desert, where dead serpents come back to life in the moonlight.

THE NUT-BROWN MAID

Nell was certainly the perfect companion for adventures. She was as brave and as vigorous as a boy, and more intelligent. I loved her very much and wanted to make her my mistress. But she rebuffed me.

Why? How would I know, having never had the time to study women? Besides, women get on my nerves. I understand nothing of their ways. I prefer wild animals. At least they let you catch them, and once you've caught them, that's it, there's no going back. But women, good Lord! ... Once you've got them, you have to keep hold of them. And you cannot keep hold of them. You should be especially careful when they say they love you. When they don't say anything, then it's possible that they like you. But even then, it's not certain. When they say they detest you, chances are that it isn't true. But it is perhaps also an inadvertent admission of the secret hatred that every woman, whether consciously or unconsciously, harbours against men. Now I'm talking like a book. All that, just to reiterate that at the end of the day, anything is possible with women, and nothing is certain.

I'm not cunning, me. As a result, I have not been taken in as often as those who are. You must not be cunning with women. They always notice it, but they are cleverer than you and so pretend not to have seen anything. Thus, without your knowing a thing, they'll put on a remarkable little act for you. And you're fooled by it. I really pity the men who boast of their female conquests. They must have been cuckolded without ever knowing it, the poor things!

Nell was not a real woman, and yet she wasn't ugly. She had a beautiful brow and beautiful eyelids. I love long, arched feet and long, thin hands. I detest little feet that are incapable of endless walks, and little hands that cannot handle revolvers or rifles. In general, women are quite a nuisance. But Nell was not a real woman.

I do not know why she didn't want to be my mistress. We don't have morals in the woods, but she was resistant to love. There are many women who have an instinctive loathing of men. It wasn't that she had a profound hatred for me – on the contrary, she had declared her fraternal love for me. When I wounded my hand, she tended to me better than a nun. She even consoled me, with all sorts of friendly, gentle words.

'My poor old boy,' she repeated, though I was only thirty years old at the time …

I will never forget her eyes, which were brown as hazelnuts, and her short hair, the colour of sand. I called her the Nut-Brown Maid,[7] in memory of an old Scottish ballad. She too was a virgin, and brown as a hazelnut.

As I was saying, she loved me very much, as a friend, as a comrade and as a hunting companion. But when I tried to make her feel the sneaking desire that had gradually crept into my veins, I came up against her willpower, as unbending as an iron wall. At those moments, she looked at me with such wild horror in her eyes and with such complete, suddenly hostile repulsion that I had to beat a retreat. The only things she liked were the outdoors, walks through the forest, wildflowers gathered along the path, and danger and adventure. She was made for danger and adventure as much as I was. We loved one another like brothers. At the heart of our friendship, no matter how real, was the putrid slime of suspicion, of hatred, even. She distrusted me, and I could not forget my fierce resentment of being a spurned male. Men are pigs, you know, simple pigs; indeed, it is their only advantage over women, who are sometimes weak enough to make the mistake of being good … I will never forgive Nell for not wanting to be my mistress … I will never forgive her, not even on my deathbed.

One incident upset me particularly. We were in the middle of the forest one green evening, when I tried to kiss her on the mouth. She punched me between the eyes with such tremendous force that I was disfigured for more than two weeks … Two weeks during which my hunting companions teased me mercilessly. But that wasn't all. She added insult to the physical injury she had caused.

'I would rather eat a toad than let you kiss me,' she said, pointing to the minuscule brown beast that had invited the unflattering comparison.

I had an idea – a rather cowardly one, I admit, but an ingenious one nevertheless. Still in great pain, I engaged in a frantic chase, which resulted in the capture of the little toad.

'Eat it right away,' I ordered, 'or I'll kiss you by force.'

She looked me in the eye. She was solemn, realising that I was not joking. An expression of unutterable contempt twisted her thin lips, the lips of an ascetic and a recluse. She picked up the horrid little beast and ate it, turning only a little paler. The trifling deed disheartened me. I no longer tried to kiss her – and I held a deadly grudge against her.

One day, she came to me, her hazelnut eyes clearer and more joyful than usual.

'I have a superb plan to propose to you, dear old Jerry.[8] You know I have infinite affection for you, even though I chose to eat a toad rather than kiss you. I am going to prove my friendship by taking you with me this evening. We will set off at sundown in a little boat. We will take a torch to light our way. And we will hunt by that magnificent light, just the two of us. We will kill lots of deer before the morning.'

'I'd like that,' I agreed. And that very evening, we embarked in a little boat that an old Indian had loaned to Nell.

What unforgettable magnificence! The torch soaked the river with bloody scarlet reflections. You would have thought there was a flaming palace in the water. The banks burst forth in blood red. The trees grew red leaves, as if it were October … It was as beautiful as a scene from hell, except that in the place of the damned, there was only me. And I do not believe that I had committed a monumental-enough sin to deserve that splendid show.

'Over there!' Nell whispered urgently. With her outstretched finger, she pointed to the right bank. I saw two large eyes reflecting the red light.

'A deer!' I exulted. I seized my rifle, and, aiming between the two luminous eyes, I fired. We heard a rustling of leaves and reeds, and then the water was stirred by something heavy falling.

Nell let out a cry of joy when we discovered a superb deer on the surface, which I grabbed by the antlers and hauled triumphantly into the boat.

Nell took hold of the oars again, and we went down the river in silence.

It was a beautiful yellow night. The shadows looked like thick layers of amber. The moonlight was streaming down like molten gold lava. And the stars at the bottom of the river were sparkling like the spangles of a harlequin's tunic.

Something sentimental was foolishly crying out within me. If the business with the toad hadn't been still running through my mind, I would have loved Nell at that moment, with passionate tenderness. I am no good at expressing myself in words, but I would have taken her hand in mine, and I would have become a better person. I would have no longer felt any anger or hatred for anyone. I would have forgiven the Indian who stole my silver watch. I would have even forgiven *her* for the idiotic love that was causing me pain. I would have become credulous and trusting, like a little child. I would have performed worthy, altruistic deeds, for her and because of her. I would have helped people. I would have stopped fighting, even with the Tuscaroras. To get closer to her, I would have become gentle like her. Yes, I would have stopped being brave in order to be good, and isn't that the greatest sacrifice one can make for a woman?

In the shadows I could make out Nell's beautiful forehead and beautiful lowered eyelids. I could feel myself becoming as stupid as a poetry book, calling myself an idiot all the while.

The low voice of the Nut-Brown Maid interrupted my hopeless reverie.

'Those eyes staring at us through the bushes! Have you seen those eyes, Jerry?[9] They are not the eyes of a deer ... They shine completely differently, and they are smaller and set further apart ... Do you see them, over there? How they are shining through the bushes!'

'You're right, Nell.'

'And look at how they're moving! Deers' eyes don't move like that. Deer don't move their heads in irregular circles like that. Their eyes dart quickly from one thing to the next, or stare intently

... Deer don't have such indecisive, flickering eyes, Jerry.'

My rifle disturbed the river and the night with a brief clap of thunder.

Nell cried, 'Don't shoot, idiot!' But it was too late. The shot was fired.

We looked towards the bank. To my great surprise, the eyes were still staring at us through the bushes. But they were shining with a red glimmer of anger. I turned to Nell, expecting an explanation for this mystery.

We heard what sounded like the grunt of a furious pig. I felt myself turn pale. Even the Nut-Brown Maid was slightly flustered.

It was a grizzly bear ...

'Your bullet must have hit him,' whispered Nell. 'Let's hope he doesn't attack us!'

The crunch of leaves ... An abrupt, heavy dive ... Nell's fears were becoming a reality. The bear was swimming after us.

With all her strength and all her courage, Nell pushed the boat forward. We glided rapidly over the river, followed by the sniffing and snorting bear.

We were enveloped in the uncertainty of night.

'If he catches up with us,' said Nell, very calmly, 'his weight will capsize the boat. We'll have to swim, like the bear – and one of us will not make it to the bank.'

Naturally, I hoped that it would be she ... We were unarmed. Our rifles had slid to the bottom of the boat, and the water had rendered them useless ... And, by a diabolical stroke of bad luck, I couldn't locate my knife. I turned towards the young woman, whose paddle was cutting tirelessly through the water. Suddenly, she stood up with a nervous jump.

'Listen, Jerry ...'

Our apprehensive eyes met. We heard the sound of falling water.

'It must be the waterfall we heard higher up, at the bend of the river,' I ventured.

'No ... The sound of water is close. Jerry, Jerry, the waterfall is no longer one hundred metres away ... Use the butt of your rifle as an oar and help me stop the boat.'

We had managed to slow the skiff down, and were hoping to steer it towards the bank, when a heavy crash rocked the back of the boat. The light of the flickering torch revealed the head and the long, curved claws of the bear. The tenacious creature was not at all discouraged by the unsteady boat, which was frantically dancing and threatening to flip bottom-up, but it did give us a moment of respite.

Nell looked at me with her indomitable eyes.

'Are you afraid, Jerry? I am not afraid ... Perhaps it will be very brief ... I've always had a lot of affection for you, my brother Jerry.'

A surge of love, violent as despair, pushed me towards her.

'Since we are both going to die, my dear, my beloved ... Since we are going to die in ten minutes, in five minutes, in three minutes, perhaps ... Give me your lips ... Let me kiss you on the mouth ... And I will die happier than I have lived. I will even be content to die.'

She was as hostilely pure as one of those little sea animals that live hidden inside a mother-of-pearl shell ... I saw her whole brown face tense with pain.

'I can't, Jerry. Even faced with the great darkness, I can't ... And yet, I love you very much, my brother Jerry ...'

This was even more bitter than the prospect of death ...
Admittedly, I was very stupid that evening, even more so than
usual.

She quickly pulled herself together.

'All is not lost, Jerry. We must not die without putting up a
fight against Death.'

I replied with a disheartened gesture. 'If we land the boat,
we'll fall into the claws of the bear ... And if we don't land, the
current will carry us over the cataract ... It might be very high
... It might be fifty, or even a hundred feet high.'

'In that case, let's head for land,' Nell decided. 'In the
meantime, grab the barrel of your rifle and hit the bear on the
muzzle.'

I did as she said and we glided towards land. Suddenly, a loud
cracking sound rang out, more terrible than a revolver fired right
into the ear ... I could not hold back a cry of terror ... Nell,
silent as Bravery itself, showed me the useless broken handle of
the paddle.

'Swim for it!' I cried.

'It's too late, Jerry ...'

The overpowering current was pulling us towards the cataract.

Sitting in the darkness and in the shadow of death, we looked
at each other one last time. I would carry the bitterness of her
quiet refusal with me into the unknown.

'Oh, how cold Death is!' Nell shivered.

What a horrible memory! ... The little boat leapt forward. It
was the abominable waterfall ... Noise ... Water ... Foam ...
Water like dust or smoke ... The spray and the steam ... The
darkness ...

... And the reawakening.

We were gently floating on very calm water. The thunder of the cataract was now but an echo. Nell, eyelids lowered, seemed to be collecting her thoughts.

My head was spinning like a child's ball. The stupor into which I was plunged was like the painful daze the day after drinking heavily.

'Nell ...' I called, very quietly.

She slowly lifted her beautiful eyelids.

I could think only of stupid words.

'It was just a little waterfall, after all ... If only I had known ... And the bear?'

We saw it in the yellow darkness, swimming towards the bank. The fright of the unexpected drop had taken his mind off his anger. He had decided to abandon his vengeance and head for the safety of the shore.

'There are idiots who say you only die once, Jerry ... But I will have experienced two deaths ...'

SAPPHO ENCHANTS THE SIRENS

The woman who embodied my destiny, the woman who first revealed me to myself, took me by the hand. She took me by the hand and led me to the grotto where the songs of Sappho enchant the Sirens.

Just as the Goddess once hid in the depths of the Venusberg and reigned there, despite the turning centuries and the changing universe, so the *musiciennes* took refuge in a Mediterranean grotto. The blue stalactites glitter distantly there like frozen stars. The sea whispers around the rocks, rocks whose green-algae hair is bejewelled with anemones. Foam breaks upon walls more polished than marble.

'Come,' said the virgin who embodied my destiny. 'But remember that those who enter the grotto may never return among the living.

'Like these women here, you will be for ever under the spell of the past. The waves will muffle the far-off clamour of the masses. The blue-green shadows of evening will make you scorn the light of day. You will become a stranger to the race of man. Their joys will be unknown to you; their criticisms will be of no importance to you. You will remain apart until the end of your earthly days. You will be more dead than the gleaming phantoms that surround you and guard the uncertain legacy of the Illustrious Ones.

'Sappho will extend to you the flower of her graces. Erinna will tell you of Agatharchis and Myro. Nossis will weave for you her mauve irises. Telesilla will sing the praises of valiant heroines.

Anyta will evoke in her pastoral verses the coolness of fountains and the shadows of orchards. Moiro will trouble you with her enigmatic Byzantine gaze. The past, louder and more alive than the present, will catch you in its silvery nets. You will be held captive by dreams and lost harmonies. But you will breathe the violets of Sappho and the crocuses of Erinna of Telos. You will gaze upon the white peploses of the virgins who bend to gather shells as delicately mysterious as a naked sex. Sometimes, seated on a rock, they listen to the marine soul of the conches. Towards evening, the Kitharedes will sing for them the songs of their native lands. Come!'

And I heard a chord like a sunset breeze whispering through the pines of evening ...

My strange companion took me by the hand, and I followed her into the grotto where Sappho enchants the Sirens.

THE HELL CLUB

The Glasgow Hell Club,[10] says the English authoress Mrs Crowe in a curious volume, *The Night Side of Nature*, was the talk of that fine Puritan town. Its orgies were harshly criticised by the modern disciples of John Knox, who shook their respectable Scotch heads in unison.

The Hell Club met every night. These evenings went on until the wee hours of the morning. And the few passers-by awake at dawn would gaze upon the still-illuminated windows of the Club, concealing their vague fear. The lights were softer and spectral in the vast, reproving brightness of day. Raucous songs snaked upwards, interspersed with drunken hiccoughs. And horrible laughter burst forth, as sinister as loveless kisses.

Every kind of low and vile debauchery was avidly sought out by members of the demoniacal Club. They were hated by the fearful and despised by the cautious. All drew back as they passed insolently by.

The most cynical of the damned was Ninian Graham. This young Scotsman, who was neither without talent nor without prospects, was mired in the pleasures of vice. As soon as he came of age, he abandoned his studies for his mistresses Barbara and Maggie, and, unable to choose between the two of them, he spent a fortune on them both.

One November evening, Ninian headed towards the mountains. His horse was valiantly following the rocky trail that ran alongside an abyss when a stranger, who had been lying in wait behind a shadowy rock, rushed onto the path. He took hold of the animal's bridle and said 'Come!' to the young Scotsman, who was frozen with incomprehensible terror.

'Where are you taking me?' came Ninian's quavering voice, at last.

'To Hell!' replied the unknown man, of whom nothing could be seen but eyes vast as shadowy despair.

Then the unknown man pulled Ninian down into the abyss ... They fell ... They fell for an incalculable time. The unknown man finally spoke:

'We have come to the end.'

Ninian expected a ferocious clamour, blasphemy and gnashing of teeth. His sweaty brow was still. His eyelids fluttered, then closed again over his sightless eyes.

A murmur of voices woke him from his wretched stupor. He violently opened his dazed eyes.

He was in the house of his aunt, who had been dead for five or six years. The venerable old lady was knitting, while her guests of long ago – an old naval officer, a retired merchant and his respectable wife – played bezique. Ninian recognised them all. He shivered. They had the air of honesty and blissful happiness that, during their earthly existence, had been their principal attraction.

'Where am I, then?' stammered the young man.

'In Hell,' answered his old aunt, quite simply. And, smiling, she once more lowered her eyes to her work.

An unspeakable horror took hold of Ninian and gnawed at the marrow of his bones. In a fierce rush, he reached the door, ran down the stairs and hurled himself into the street.

The Presbyterian clocks of a Scottish Sunday were steadily

ringing. A well-dressed crowd of people were leaving church. Among them were fathers of families, important patronesses of charities, retired grocers and magistrates. Young women went past, their hair unbelievably neat, holding well-disciplined children by the hand.

'Where am I, then?' Ninian asked one of the irreproachable wives.

'In Hell,' they all answered, in voices both modest and assured.

Ninian wandered the crowded streets for a long time. Night fell, perfectly misty, and a vespertine peace hung over the houses. The young man saw the red glow of a cabaret shining through the shadows. There were men singing and drinking. Whisky gilded their goblets and gin silvered their cups like lunar water. Their fine drunken faces reassured and comforted Ninian.

'Where am I, then?' he asked an old drunkard, who was cheerfully launching into an obscene ditty.

'In Hell, *damn you*,'[11] the jovial fellow shot back, with a hearty laugh. His cordial demeanour gave the traveller new heart.

'I've always been told that Hell is a place of unbelievable torture,' he remarked. 'People must be mistaken, or – though I doubt it very much – I am myself mistaken.'

'They are not mistaken, and nor are you,' the drunkard interrupted. 'We are very cheerful in Hell. That is why we suffer so abominably.'

'But from what I can see,' Ninian objected, 'everyone here is just reliving their earthly life.'

'And that is the agony,' replied the drunk. He paused to knock back a large, amber-coloured glass of brandy, and then went on tearfully: 'We were all souls with neither love nor vision. We sought only egotistical material satisfaction. Thus we are

89

condemned to relive our past lives for eternity. We retain, as we did in life, an innocent gaze and a serene brow. We lead, as we did in life, the satisfied existence of good, honest folk. And only we know what lies in our hearts and minds. We were the honest folk who, proud of our blameless pasts, unforgivingly judged the faults of our neighbours. We were the good folk who, in the placidity of our wealth, remained insensible to the sufferings of others. We were the rapacious and voracious good folk who were imitated deferentially by those around us. We were the ferocious and stupid honest folk who observed decorum and maintained the laws. And that is why we are condemned to eternal punishment.' Drunken tears trickled down his purplish cheeks.

He gets depressed when he's had a few, thought Ninian.

The smoke was so thick that it shrouded the misty faces. The bitter fumes of alcohol, bad breath and sweat got into Ninian's throat and suffocated him ... He tottered on his legs, trembling and staggering.

He found himself on the moors, his head buried in the heather. His horse was grazing several feet away. The morning air stung his cheeks and temples.

According to all evidence, the dream was a premonition from Heaven, since, a year and a day after this strange vision, Ninian Graham died – without having made amends, alas!

The mistakes of his earthly life were such that we cannot hope he obtained divine mercy. He could not, or rather, he did not know how to, escape the Hell that had been so miraculously revealed to him.

THE FRIENDSHIP OF WOMEN

Of all the heavy-handed idiocies that Philistines of letters inflict upon their readers, this is, I think, the most astounding:

'Women are incapable of friendship. There has never been a David and Jonathan among women.'

Might I suggest that David's affection for Jonathan has always seemed to me more passionate than brotherly? I need no further evidence than the young conqueror's funeral oration:

I am distressed for thee, my brother Jonathan: very pleasant hast thou been unto me: thy love to me was wonderful, passing the love of women.

I do not believe that this passage springs from the pallid tears of mournful friendship. I see in it rather the bloody tears of a widowed lover.

How much more disinterested is the magnificent tenderness of Ruth the Moabite for Naomi! No carnal languor could have crept into the friendship between the two women. Naomi was no longer young. She herself says: 'I am too old to have a husband.'

I know of nothing as simple, beautiful or touching as this passage:

And she said, Behold, thy sister-in-law is gone back unto her people, and unto her gods: return thou after thy sister-in-law.

And Ruth said, Intreat me not to leave thee, or to return from following after thee: for whither thou goest I will go: and where thou lodgest, I will lodge: thy people shall be my people, and thy God, my God:

Where thou diest, will I die, and there will I be buried: the Lord do so to me, and more also, if aught but death part thee and me.

Like the most beautiful music, these words leave you face to face with the Infinite, speechless and breathless.

Upon the resigned offer of Naomi, whom the Almighty is sending back *empty* to her native country, Ruth the Moabite responds with that sentence of imploring humility: *Intreat me not to leave thee, or to return from following after thee.* Like a whispering prelude before the full organ, these words prepare for the incomparable strophe: *Whither thou goest, I will go ...*

No sob of passionate love has ever equalled this fervour, nor this selflessness. It is here that the poetry of friendship surpasses the poetry of love. It is absolute devotion, pure passion. And this tenderness extends beyond the grave: *Where thou diest, will I die, and there will I be buried.*

Be honoured then, Naomi, whose name signifies 'beauty and sweetness', for the friendship you inspired in your daughter-in-law, celebrated thus by the virgins of Israel:

Thy daughter-in-law, which loveth thee, which is better to thee than seven sons ...

In truth, the Book of Ruth is the apotheosis of magnanimous friendship. Friendship, the chaste fusion of souls, melting snow upon fallen snow ... Friendship, the sobbing of citharas and the perfume of violets ...

Believe me, oh Naomis and Ruths of the future: friendship is the best and the sweetest aspect of love.

SVANHILD

A Prose Piece

Scene I

(The scene represents one of the banks in Nordfjord. There are mountains in the distance. Several young women dressed in peasant costume form a moving group; they are treading upon bluebells, thyme and gentians. Svanhild, motionless on a rock, gazes into the distance.)

THORUNN

What are you staring at, Svanhild? And what do you await in silence every day?

SVANHILD

I am awaiting the return of the wild swans.

GUDRID

You know very well that they have not come back to this land since the day you were born. They stopped and rested for a long time on the roof of the house that sheltered you. As long as the light lasted, they lingered on that mossy roof with its blue and gold flowers and then, at dusk, they flew away with a great beating of wings.

SVANHILD

They will return.

BERGTHORA

It has been twenty years since they flew north, and since that day, not one of us has seen them fly past.

SVANHILD

I know they will return.

BERGTHORA

Why do you stand on the rock, motionless and contemplative, for whole days at a time?

SVANHILD

I am awaiting the return of the wild swans.

(Festive songs are heard. Boats go past on the fjord, laden with women clad in sparkling costumes.)

PEASANT WOMEN

(Singing)

Do not go near the glacier

For the cold sears like the flame.

Do not go near the snowfield,

For the snow blinds like the sun.

(Moving away.)

Do not linger too long upon the peaks,

For their haze can daze the mind.

Do not contemplate the chasm,

For its depths can drown like wells.

HILDEGUND

Listen to that faraway music. The boats glide across the fjord, rocking gently. The peasants row and sing: they are happy.

SVANHILD

Their joys would be for me the greatest torment, and my joys would be for them the most dreadful torture.

GUDRID

Do you like nothing on earth?

SVANHILD

I like whiteness.

THORUNN

What gift do you hope for from life in the springtime?

SVANHILD

Whiteness.

ERMENTRUDE

If fate miraculously grants your wish and the wild swans return, what will you do then?

SVANHILD

I will follow them.

BERGTHORA

How far will you follow them?

SVANHILD

All the way to the setting sun.

HILDIGUNN

What do you want from your dream?

SVANHILD

More whiteness.

Scene II

(A passing woman enters, her arms full of flowers, her head bare, her hair mingled with thyme and blades of grass.)

THE PASSING WOMAN

The roads are gloriously wide. I am drunk on the dust of the path. I slept on the heather, and in my dreams inhaled the perfume of the mountaintops. Red and violet berries satisfied my hunger, and melted snow slaked my thirst. I gathered roses from the mountainsides. I danced naked under the sun. Is there anything more beautiful under the springtime sky than the lizards on the rocks, the blue and lavender thistles, the sparkling glimpse of fish and the shades of evening?

SVANHILD

There is something more beautiful.

THE WOMAN

What on earth can be more beautiful?

SVANHILD

Clouds, snow, smoke and foam.

THE WOMAN

Have you no desire to follow the road, free as the horizon and as immense as the dawn, by my side?

SVANHILD

No.

THE WOMAN

Why not?

SVANHILD

I am awaiting the return of the wild swans.

(The woman goes joyously on her way.)

Scene III

(The sun is sinking. The setting sun illuminates the sky. The evening is pale and grey.)

BERGTHORA

Evening is here. How mysterious the mountains are!

GUDRID

How strange the silence is!

HILDIGUNN

The universe seems to be waiting.

SVANHILD

(To herself.)

Waiting … like me.

THORUNN

Death lies in wait for the lost souls who linger in the mountains.

ASGERD

The paths are perilous when the fog rolls down from the peaks.

SVANHILD

(With a loud cry.)

The swans! The swans! The swans!

ALL

(Looking into the distance.)

We cannot see anything.

SVANHILD

The northern wind blows through their wings ... They must have crossed the sea, for foam silvers their feathers. They are heading for the open ocean. Their wings are spread wide and are quivering like sails ... Do you not hear the generous beating of their wings?

ALL

We can see only the white clouds that float above the fjord.

SVANHILD

They are more beautiful than the clouds. They are flying towards the Northern Lights. They are more beautiful than the snow. How powerful and sonorous their flight is! Do you not hear them flying past?

ALL

We can hear only the evening breeze upon the waters of the fjord.

SVANHILD

I will follow them! I will follow them all the way to the setting sun!

ASGERD

Svanhild! The paths are perilous when the fog rolls down from the peaks.

THORUNN

Death lies in wait for the lost souls who linger in the mountains.

GUDRID

Think of the dense fog that obscures the chasms.

SVANHILD

Oh, whiteness!

(She disappears into the mist.)

ASGERD

She will get lost in the twilight.

GUDRID

She will perish in the night. Svanhild!

ALL

(Calling.)

Svanhild!

ECHO

Svanhild!

(A loud cry, which echoes and re-echoes, is heard.)

GUDRID

(With horror.)

The chasm ...

AS WHITE AS FOAM

As white as the foam upon the grey of the rocks, Andromeda looked out at the sea, and her gaze was burning with desire for Space.

Under the weight of her golden chains, her delicate limbs were bathed in sunlight. The wind of the open sea blew through her flowing hair. The laughter of the sea carried towards her, and the dazzling glare of the glittering waves entered her soul.

She was waiting for Death; she was waiting, as white as the foam upon the grey of the rocks.

She already felt lost in the infinite, at one with the horizon and the gold-tinted waves, with the distant mists, with the entire atmosphere and all its resounding clarity. She did not fear chaste-eyed, solemn-handed Death. She feared only Love, which ravages the spirit and the flesh.

As white as the foam upon the grey of the rocks, she considered that in delivering her virginal body to virginal Death, the merciful gods were sparing her the bitterness and corruption of the implacable Eros.

Her eyes suddenly widened as they fixed on the Sea Monster, who was coming towards his motionless prey from afar – towards his royal victim.

His glaucous scales were streaming with blue and green water, and glistening with flashes of light. He was magnificent and astonishing. And his huge eyes were as deep as the ocean that soothed him with its rhythms and its dreams.

A sob of terror and love burst from Andromeda's lips. Her eyelids fluttered, before closing at the exquisite pleasure of his gaze. Upon her lips was the bitter taste of Death.

But the hour of deliverance had come, and the hero appeared like a bolt of summer lightning, armed by the Olympians. The battle took place in the waves, and Perseus's sword was victorious. The Monster sank slowly into the shadowy waters.

Just as the triumphant Perseus was breaking the captive's golden chains, the silent reproach in her tears caused him to pause.

And Andromeda slowly sobbed: 'Why could you not let me perish in the grandeur of sacrifice? The beauty of my incomparable destiny intoxicated me, and now you have robbed me of the Lethean kiss. O Perseus, understand that only the Sea Monster knew my sob of desire, and that Death was to me less melancholy than your impending embrace.'

BONA DEA

The day is dying. It is the spring evening devoted to the Good Goddess, Bona Dea. Cover the picture of my father with an impenetrable veil, so the gaze of the Immortal Virgin is not offended by the sight of a man.

Tonight, my father's house will be the temple in which the sacred rites are carried out ...

How beautiful the statue of the Daughter of Faunus is! Bona Dea, deign to lower your smiling eyes to our choirs and offerings. I wove with my own hands the crown of violets that will be placed upon your head ... How vast and solemn your marble brow is, oh Goddess!

Here is the golden vase into which I poured the wine of Lesbos. The wine is as luminous as Peitho's locks. It is as purple as Apollo's cloak. It will delight the dancing souls of the intertwined women.

Amata, thrice precious, close your beautiful eyelids, which are like dusky flowers. Abandon your childlike hands to my ardent ones.

I love you. I, Caia Venantia Paullina, daughter of Caius Venantius Paullinus, love you, my little Gallic slave. You were but a sickly, graceless child whom the merchants despised. But I immediately cherished you fervently for your languor and your fragility. I opened my arms to you, to console you as much as to embrace you ...

For I am the one who rules and protects. I love you with a

105

sweet and imperious love. I love you as both a lover and a sister. You will obey me, my sweet burden, but you may do with me all that you wish. I will be both your master and your possession. I love you with the frenzy of male desire and with the languor of female tenderness.

I once opened my arms to you, to console you as much as to embrace you. I was enchanted by the innocence of your shivering naked body, though I did not yet lust after it. I loved you for your trembling, fragile self. My strength was drawn to your weakness. For I am the one who rules and protects.

And now you are beautiful, Amata. Your breasts, like polished stones, are firm and cool to the touch. Your green eyes reflect the emerald leaves of oak trees. Your white skin is as translucent as mistletoe berries. Your flowing hair shines with the splendour of forests in October.

And because you are so beautiful, Amata; because you are the most graceful of young women, I will reveal to you the potency and sweetness of female love.

If you deliver your consenting body to me, I will teach you the manifold art of pleasure. I will teach you the deliberate slowness of hands that linger over belated contact. I will teach you the tenacity of lips that delicately persist. You will discover the all-consuming power of a gentle caress.

When you were but a graceless, sickly child, I taught you the odes of Sappho of Lesbos, whose beautiful Doric name is Psappha. Know, my beautiful slave, that Psappha, reclining among the Lethean lotuses, smiles when I call upon her, and extends her protection over my love affairs, because I am her priestess. She will help me conquer and capture your undecided heart, Amata.

I love you just as Psappha once loved the elusive, hesitant Atthis.

Because you are the most graceful of young women, Amata, I will reveal to you the potency and sweetness of love between women.

You are free, my beautiful slave! Here is the linen robe I wove for you ... It is white, Amata, and it invites touch just as your body does. You are free. You may leave this house which protected you in childhood. You may return to your own land, and I will neither blame you nor reproach you, nor will I darken your joy with a single complaint.

For the love between women is nothing like the love of men. I love you for you, and not for myself. I desire only the smile upon your lips and the radiance of your gaze.

Why am I beautiful in your eyes? For it is you who are beautiful, not I. My hair does not have the evening gold of your hair. My eyes do not have the distant clarity of your eyes. My lips do not have the fine shape of your lips. In truth, it is you who are beautiful, not I.

Never have I seen a virgin as desirable as you, oh, my voluptuous, languorous beauty! ... Next to you, I am not beautiful at all. If you are tempted by a more charming virgin, take her. I desire only the smile upon your lips.

I love you.

My pearls will shine more lustrously around your neck. My beryls will be clearer upon your arms. Take my necklaces. Take my rings, too. Then you will be ready for the feast of Bona Dea.

The Goddess is humble and sweet and forgiving to women. She hates men, because they are ferocious and brutal. Men love only their pride or their brutishness. They are neither just nor loyal. They are sincere only about their own vanity. But the Goddess is all truth and justice. She is as full of pity as the water that refreshes our lips and the sun that warms our limbs. She is the merciful spirit of the universe.

It was she who made the first flowers grow. Flowers are an act of love from Bona Dea, a symbol of Her favour for mortal women.

She loves only the faces of women. No man may sully with his presence the venerable temple in which she delivers her oracles. And only the priestesses have heard the divine sound of her voice.

She is the Daughter of Faunus. She is the prophetic and chaste Fauna. But her secret name, which must never be uttered by the profane lips of man, I will quietly reveal to you: it is Oma. Do not divulge this sacred name.

The day is dying. It is the spring evening devoted to the Good Goddess. With their chaste hands, the Vestal Virgins have garlanded the walls that are perfumed by the foliage.

Is this not what you would call a motionless forest? ... The last lights of day linger upon your pale hair ... You resemble a hamadryad framed by shadows and greenery ...

With their chaste hands, the Vestal Virgins have garlanded the walls that are perfumed by the foliage. They have chosen the simple flowers and the herbs most beloved of Fauna: balm, thyme, chervil, fennel and parsley. And here are the hyacinths ... And here are the roses ...

Bona Dea is contented with the joy of the universe. The pitiful nymphs serve her and honour her, the nymphs who in feverish summers carry in the palms of their hands a water sweeter than honey ...

The Goddess has coloured the apple trees crimson. She

has made the virginal garden crocus gold. She has turned the nocturnal-blue violets purple.

Fauna smiles upon the love of the intertwined women. That is why the women will kiss at nightfall in front of her lovely statue, moulded so carefully by Theano, the Greek woman. Her hair is made of solid gold, her limbs of ivory and her eyes of emerald. But your hair is even more luminous, and your limbs more polished, and your eyes more intensely green ...

My fervent hands placed a crown of vine leaves upon her divine head. A serpent is coiled at her delicate feet. For she who is Eternal Gentleness is also Eternal Wisdom.

The wives who are coming tonight have purified themselves by refusing the carnal embraces of their husbands. But they are less dear to the Goddess than the sacred virgins.

Night is upon us, azure as the veil that protects the divine image and that may only be removed by the hands of the priestesses. For the Goddess may only be unveiled on a spring evening when the intertwined women are piously united.

Come, Amata, my beautiful slave. If you love me a little, you will grant me the kiss that my anxious lips await from your lips. You will bend to my wilful embrace. You will abandon yourself to my imploring caress ...

But I will not importune you with my desire, nor my tenderness, Beloved. I want only the smile upon your lips.

NOTES

1. Most sources agree that these initials stand for Helene Louise Charlotte Bettina – the first names of the Baroness van Zuylen de Nyevelt (*née* Rothschild), one of Vivien's lovers.

2. Wine seller.

3. Beater.

4. 'It's still twitching its tail.'

5. Charles Cros, 1842–88, a poet and inventor who contributed to the development of the phonograph and of colour photography.

6. The crocodilian is also referred to as an alligator in the original.

7. 'The Nut-Brown Maid' is in English in the original.

8. The words 'dear old Jerry' are in English in the original.

9. The narrator is referred to as Dirk here in the original, presumably an error on the part of Vivien or her publisher. The protagonist in 'Forest Betrayal' is called Dirk.

10. These words are in English in the original.

11. In English in the original.